D1479119

Also by David Rees
from Knights Press

ISLANDS

WATERSHED

T·H·E
WRONG
APPLE

DAVID REES

Knights
Press

Stamford, Connecticut

Designed by Graphic Arts Associates
Cover photo by Gordon Micunis

Published by Knights Press, P.O. Box 454, Pound Ridge, NY 10576
Distributed by Lyle Stuart, Inc.

Library of Congress Cataloguing-in-Publication Data

Rees, David, 1936–
    The wrong apple.

    I. Title.
PR6068.E368W7 1987   823'.914   87–17083
ISBN 0–915175–25–8

Printed in the United States of America

Excerpt from MURDER IN THE CATHEDRAL by T.S. Eliot, copyright © 1935
by Harcourt Brace Janovich, Inc.; renewed 1963 by T.S. Eliot.
Reprinted by permission of the publisher.

Excerpt from "Skunk Hour" from LIFE STUDIES by Robert Lowell,
copyright © 1956, 1959 by Robert Lowell. Reprinted by permission of
Farrar, Straus and Giroux, Inc., and of Faber and Faber Ltd.

For

Peter Robins

A car radio bleats
'Love, O careless love . . . .' I hear
My ill-spirit sob in each blood cell,
As if my hand were at its throat . . . .
I myself am hell.
　　　　　—Robert Lowell, *Skunk Hour*

T·H·E
WRONG
APPLE

« ONE »

If you weren't here at this moment, where would you rather be?"

It was a strange question, considering where I was and in what situation, as if, I said to myself, I was being offered the wrong kind of apple. I must have looked puzzled, for Kim went on: "I was talking about gardens, David."

I wasn't sure if he was talking about gardens, but I decided to pick up his cue. Or clue. "There are finer examples," I said, looking round at the wilderness of trees and flowering shrubs. If I stood up, I would be reminded that it was a small wilderness, its edges carefully cultivated. The evening lights of downtown San Jose—ugly suburban sprawl—would be clearly visible. "Oh . . . the best in the world are said to be the gardens of the El Generalife in Spain. The summer residence of the Moorish kings who built the Alhambra in the thirteenth century. I've never seen them, but I'm told there are fountains, waterfalls, terraces . . .

So twice five miles of fertile ground
With walls and towers were girdled round:
And here were gardens bright with sinuous rills,
Where blossomed many an incense-bearing tree;
And here were forests—"

I stopped, for the quotation had made Kim's face go shut. He had probably never heard of the El Generalife, let alone Samuel Taylor Coleridge or *Kubla Khan.* In his brief twenty-one years, San Francisco, not quite sixty miles off, was the furthest he'd been.

"But I'm content with the gardens of Los Gatos," I said. I was. It was a perfect summer dusk, the sunset a thin wash of orange above the Santa Cruz Mountains. Bats lazily flapped, and the crickets had just started their soothing night music. If we kept very still, the mild-eyed deer—a buck, his two wives and their one little bambi— would emerge from the trees, pale grey shapes almost not there, almost figments of the imagination. Phlox scents. California lilac, long past its best, its vivid blue petals now on the ground in bright puddles like miniature swimming pools. Oleander scents, nicotiana scents. Even the dog that belonged to the Smrkovskys, Katya's supercilious neighbours, was silent: this neglected creature, permanently exiled from the house, often howled like a banshee, sometimes at four o'clock in the morning. Katya would get up and shout "SHUUUUUUDDUPPP!!", a roar that probably disturbed the inhabitants of San Jose, let alone those of nearer Los Gatos. The dog always cringed.

"Deer!" Kim whispered.

Stupidly, I turned too fast, jogging as I did so the

wine carafe on the table. The deer melted into the night, a fade technique that recalled the Cheshire cat's disappearing grin. I wondered how they managed it; or was it a trick of the dusk, the wine?

I looked at the belladonna lilies, a yard or so away. They would soon be in full bloom, a delicate miracle of pink, often growing in the roughest ground, a path, or dry waterless earth under a bush. The El Generalife probably did not have belladonna lilies.

"I'm quite content with the gardens of Los Gatos," I repeated. Not only for the flora and fauna, the endless summer sun, the fragrant twilights, but the wine we had nearly finished, the dinner—simple, but just what I'd wanted: veal escallope, bread-crumbed and lemony, with beans picked that afternoon from Katya's garden—and Kim. Curly-haired blond jock youth: frank blue eyes and a light dusting of gold hair all over his gold skin. Before dinner we had spent yet another three quarters of an hour in the sack.

We had met last year and spent a morning in bed, but I'd been reluctant to take things any further. I was teaching at the University of San Jose at the time, just for two semesters on exchange; I'd returned to England and forgotten about him. Now, back here on vacation for six weeks I'd rediscovered him, quite by chance. I was staying at Katya's. My closest friend: though living half the world away, she and I never seemed to be able to survive without an annual fix of each other's company. Sometimes in California, sometimes in England; but we'd managed to meet in other places too, New York, Athens, and—improbably—Galway in western Ireland. Twice married, with four children grown up now and left home, she had ages ago fled from Berkeley and her alcoholic second husband to Los Gatos. It was a very good spot to flee to. This year she was teaching summer school, which meant, for me, certain days when I was alone and lonely. I was glad I'd bumped into Kim.

"How far does your garden extend?" I'd asked her. "You know, I've never explored it properly." We were looking over the fence at the Smrkovskys' baleful hound; it was five thirty on the second morning of my visit, cool, with a mist that would burn off before breakfast. The dog, of course, had woken us.

"One of these days I'm going to *kill* it," she said. "Rat poison, I think. Or a slow garrotte." She ground out her cigarette end, angrily. "I don't know how far the garden extends. I've never explored it, either."

Not so odd; it wasn't her property: she rented it. The lawn and the flowerbeds near the house she knew well of course, and looked after them lovingly. Beyond the lawn was a thicket of shrubs that dipped into a valley so overgrown it was almost invisible; there might not even be a fence in it that marked the boundary of her land, or, if there was, it could be rotten or broken, for the deer stepped warily out of the thicket at nightfall and grazed on Katya's lawn. Beautiful though she agreed they were, they were not her favourite animals, for the lawn was merely their second choice of supper menu. They preferred her sweet peas, roses, marigolds, nasturtiums, antirrhinums, fuschias and petunias, indeed anything that flowered. The only vegetation they didn't munch was the tangerine tree, but the local fraternity of humming birds regarded that as their bailiwick. "Dried lions' urine," she said to me. "That keeps the deer off, so I'm told. But how the fuck do I go into a store and ask for dried lions' urine? The clerk would fall over laughing."

"Is it dried lions, or dried urine?"

"Maybe last thing at night you could pee in the corners of the flower-beds."

"I don't think I'd have enough pee. And I'm not a lion."

She sighed. "The tribulations of a rural existence!"

"Shove off," I said. To the Smrkovskys' dog. It was poking its nose through what little fence Katya's garden did have.

"I envy the Smrkovskys that swimming pool."

"It isn't very de luxe." It was not a sunken, concrete and cement affair beside which you could be ultra-Californian and drink Almaden all day, but of the plastic, do-it-yourself variety, plonked in the middle of the lawn like an ugly water tank.

"They never use it. All the years I've been here, I've never seen anybody in it." Katya, a keen swimmer, did not own a pool, but went up the road almost daily in summer to use a friend's.

We went indoors and cooked an early breakfast. She decided to take advantage of the extra time the dog had given her, and set off at seven for the university to grade papers; I thought I'd find out where the edges of the garden really were.

There were none. All the gardens from the neighbouring houses spilled into the overgrown valley, and no fences indicated the boundaries of any of them. I plunged on through brambles, thorn bushes and ivy, afraid I'd touch poison oak. And came to a clearing in which stood the smallest cottage I'd ever seen, not really much more than a two-room shanty; but, as with every California home, there was a deck with tubs of flowers and a barbecue. It looked like a West Coast variant of the gingerbread house. If so, where was the witch?

"David. You've come back," a voice behind me said, softly. In tones of wonder and surprise. Kim, dressed in shorts and the sweat-band he was wearing the day I'd first seen him, a gilded youth mindlessly chucking a frisbee to two other gilded youths on the grass outside Los Gatos's civic centre. Over cups of coffee we caught up on a year of life. He was working as a gardener, employed by the owners of all the houses whose gardens petered out in the valley. Including Katya.

"She never told me," I said.

"Why should she? I do less work for her than for anyone else; she likes doing it herself. I just trim her hedges occasionally."

The girl he'd been hoping to marry had gone off with some other guy. "I'd have killed him," Kim said, "if I hadn't realised it was my fault."

"Your fault?"

"I couldn't go on . . . delivering the goods." He grinned, shyly. "I'm gay. Three parts gay, one part straight. Not that I've . . . gotten completely reconciled to the fact. Yet."

"So what do you do about it?"

"Drive up to San Francisco on week-ends. Then hardly ever dare risk anything . . . I don't want AIDS. I've never been in the baths. Never been fucked. You" —his grin became wider—"you're British. Safe, I guess."

I got the message. But was *he* safe? More so, I reasoned, than other Californians I was likely to find. Never been fucked, didn't dare risk anything. True? Probably. The cottage, I noticed when we went indoors, was indeed minute; just a kitchen, and a bedroom so small the double bed almost filled it. There wasn't even space for a closet: his clothes hung from a rail fixed to the ceiling. "Who owns this shack?" I asked.

"The de los Rioses." Katya's neighbours on the other side. "The rent's dirt cheap. I like it here, living by myself. Jesus! I never thought I would! But . . . it's giving me . . . uh . . . time to think things out. Peace and quiet. Though I guess I shan't be here too long."

His body was as beautiful as I remembered it, and his technique more sophisticated than a year ago: a lot of kissing, a lot of foreplay, enjoying *my* body. But when the time came to be inside me, I wondered as I did on subsequent occasions why it never hurt, for when he got going sophistication completely disappeared.

David Rees

"I hope you'll come back," he said afterwards, as we lay on the bed smoking cigarettes. "Not like last time."

"I will," I promised. And did, that evening.

Yes, quite content with the gardens of Los Gatos. Even helped him in his work when Katya was busy in school; that afternoon we'd almost sawn down a palm tree. It was a gigantic specimen, thrusting far above the other trees in the valley, the olives, eucalyptuses and live oaks; it was in the de los Rioses' garden, or so they claimed (you couldn't, in this unmarked jungle, be certain of who owned what), and it was obstructing their view. They should be grateful for that, I said to Kim; who could possibly want a *good* view of downtown San Jose? The job turned out to be much more difficult than we had thought. We had to saw at a particular angle and from a particular point, so that when it keeled over it would crash to the ground without damaging anyone's property. It was so tall it might, if cut the wrong way, ruin one of the gardens, smash a roof in, or even kill people. The point where we chose to begin (the only place, we calculated, where trees or bushes would be the sole victims when it fell) proved unbelievably tough. We sawed for hours, sweating, grumbling, cursing.

We were nearly through when he said, "That's it! Five thirty, time for a drink. We'll finish the job tomorrow."

"But you can't leave it like this!" I protested. "It isn't safe!"

"Who's going to knock it over? The deer?"

"Someone might."

"Nobody comes to this place."

"*I* did."

"Stop bitching and get me a Budweiser. I'm telling you it'll keep till tomorrow morning."

He's responsible, I said to myself. Not me. *I'm* not the gardener.

So we drank beer instead, showered together (there was a shower behind the bedroom so miniscule that when two people were in it neither could turn round), compared biceps—"sawing improves the muscles," Kim said, though I didn't think his great lumberjack arms needed any improvement—had sex, fixed dinner, drank the wine I'd brought, and discussed where we'd rather be if we weren't in the gardens of Los Gatos, which, we decided eventually, was nowhere else at all.

"Why don't you stay the night with me?" He'd asked for this, more than once. The wrong kind of apple again, perhaps: he could be falling in love with me, just as I'd dreaded he would, a year ago. I'd be in England in a matter of days, and he still here, weeding and digging. Falling in love was an absurd and unnecessary complication.

"I can't. I've told you before. Katya wouldn't like it."

"I suppose you'd rather screw *her*."

"Don't be ridiculous. You know I'm a guest in her house; I can't not sleep in it. It would be rude . . . unfriendly . . . unfair."

"She must know we fuck."

"Of course."

"Does she mind?"

"No!"

"Why isn't she entertaining you this evening?"

"She's in Palo Alto, playing bridge with three mad Irish folk-singers. Or maybe by now they're bubbling in the jacuzzi." Kim didn't know this Britishism, so I said, "Hot tub. Maybe they're all in the hot tub, playing bridge at the same time. Bidding four nude hearts!"

"And why aren't you with her?"

Questions, questions! "Because I don't play bridge. I can't stand the game."

"Impolite, isn't it, going off to play bridge and leaving her house-guest to fend for himself?"

I frowned. "Katya leads a very complicated social existence." I didn't explain what I meant, though he evidently wanted me to; the intricacies of Katya's engagement diary were not his concern, I decided.

He sulked a bit. I listened to the zillions of crickets whispering, and thought I heard twigs crack underfoot. The deer, I presumed. The sulk didn't last long: we were in bed again this side of midnight, as I'd hoped.

"I'll stay till morning," I said. "Just this once. Katya probably won't be in till after two, anyway."

Underneath him: I could see the window—it had no drapes, was a square of dim grey light. I wasn't paying it much attention; we had got to the final stretch, the sensations of ecstasy, Kim shouting, "I can't hold it any longer!"

"There's someone at the window!"

"I couldn't stop now if Jesus Christ himself was

looking!" A vicarious treat—or a profound moral earthquake?—for the interloper peering in. Did whoever it might be realise it was two men?

"He's gone."

Kim turned. "Ah . . . your imagination," he said. A while later, he slowly eased himself out of me, got off the bed and went to the door. He stared into the night. "Nobody!" I padded across and joined him on the deck.

I grabbed his arm. "The tree!" I cried. "Look at the tree!"

Not a breath of wind. Every branch, every twig was absolutely still except for the palm tree: its fronds were lashing backwards and forwards in a quite violent manner, and its trunk was swaying, this way, that way, in a steady rhythm like wipers swishing on a windshield. Kim rushed into the bedroom, pulled on his shorts and shoved his feet into his sneakers. "Fucking high school kids!" he shouted, and dashed out into the night.

This way, that way. Too late! The noise—whip cracks, and a kind of hollow groan, and a cracking as in a thousand arthritic joints or pieces of antique furniture: it began to fall. An arc through the moonlit sky, slow and almost dignified, then it hurtled out of control: whoo-oo-oooshsh! It slapped into the ground. A shriek of pain, which sounded curiously like a dog in agony, then water. Water? Crashing feet in the undergrowth, giggles— the culprits escaping. It had not fallen, I realised, in the intended area. It had been pushed at the wrong angle. It was, I thought, lying, most of it, in the Smrkovskys' garden.

I dressed, picked up the torch from where it had

been left near the barbecue, then hurried after Kim. I found myself floundering in a cascade of mud. The palm tree had demolished the Smrkovskys' swimming pool.

The events of the next half-hour were bewildering and rapid. The Smrkovskys of course were furious, shouting at the tops of their voices at Kim; they would sue, they'd have him arrested; he'd get years in jail. Mr Smrkovsky tried to hit him, but when Kim looked as if he'd defend himself, he changed his mind and ran indoors to call the police. The de los Rioses, disturbed by the brouhaha, came over, but they said nothing other than that they'd talk to their attorney in the morning. Prudent: they'd claimed it was their tree and they'd asked for it to be cut down; they guessed they might have to pick up the tab for the damages. Katya then appeared, a lot earlier than I'd expected. (The bridge, she told me, was not a success as the Irish folk-singers were drunk by ten and asleep by ten thirty.) Having grasped the situation, she tried to calm everybody down by offering cocktails. The police, when they arrived, were puzzled for a moment; they had expected a brawl, or at least a very unpleasant quarrel, and found something that resembled a midnight vodka party on the lawn. They took statements from all of us, except Katya. Mr Smrkovsky nearly lost his temper again when the police refused to arrest Kim. It was in no way certain, one of the officers said, that any of the people present could be suspected of criminal damage; the Smrkovskys should speak to their lawyer. "I want justice and compensation!" Mr Smrkovsky yelled. "And I want to see this guy"—he jabbed a finger at Kim—"clapped in the pen!"

It was only after the police and the de los Rioses had gone that Mrs Smrkovsky discovered her dog crushed beneath the tree. It was very dead. Its blood was mingling with the last of the water from the swimming pool, which had washed away a whole flower-bed and turned the lower part of the garden into a quagmire. She had hysterics at once, screaming and sobbing; she almost fainted, but Katya managed to hold her upright, a considerable achievement as Mrs Smrkovsky was a prime example of all that was unhealthy in American fast foods. Mr Smrkovsky attempted to hit Kim again, but thought twice when he saw fists raised. Anyone not totally insane would have thought twice, I guess, when seeing Kim's fists raised.

"See what you've done!" he shouted. "My swimming pool, my garden . . . my wife gone crazy . . . and you've killed my dog!"

"I'm glad!" Kim said. "Your fucking dog keeps the whole neighbourhood awake! I'm glad it's dead!" He kicked it, which was somewhat unnecessary in my opinion.

"I'll get him away," I said to Katya. "I'll see you in a while. Can you cope?"

"Yes." Her arms were full of Mrs Smrkovsky.

"Come on," I said to Kim, dragging him by the elbow. "Time we weren't here."

We slopped our way into the wilderness, and when we arrived back at the cottage, stripped and showered to get the mud off our skins. "Well!" he said. "At least we shan't have to cut that tree down tomorrow. And we

won't ever again be woken up by that fucking dog." I
didn't answer. "I'm glad it's dead," he repeated. "Horrible mangy brute! Aren't you glad?"

"Not particularly."

"You Brits are so dumb about pets."

"It's not the dog's fault."

"Many a time I could have kicked its balls in. Wish I
had." He grabbed at my cock. "Let's get into bed."

"No."

He stared at me. "I thought you were staying the
night."

"I've changed my mind."

"What for? What on earth for?"

Katya's at home, I could have said, but I didn't; I
told another truth. "I don't like your feelings about that
dog. You should be sorry it's dead. I am. Let alone any
responsibility you might have for leaving that tree in a
dangerous state."

I wanted to double up to protect myself: he looked so
angry. But all I could do in that tiny shower was tense my
stomach muscles. He didn't smash me into smithereens,
however. "Get out of here, " he said. "And don't imagine
for one minute I have to rely on *you* when I need to fuck."

Katya was alone on her deck, drinking vodka, a thoughtful expression on her face. "Help yourself," she said,
waving at the bottle. I did so. "You didn't stop long with
him, then. I guess I'm not too surprised."

"Why?"

"You don't care for his attitude to the dog. Any more than I do . . . whatever I might have said about poisoning it."

I laughed. "You can read me like a book! You always did."

She laughed too. "Just as you read me."

"Oh . . . Katya!" I took a large sip of vodka and orange. "Old friends . . . they're better than lovers, any day of the week!"

"Yes, you're absolutely right. But . . . *any* day of the week?"

"Well . . . perhaps one should allow the lover an occasional hour."

Which is what happened. Kim soon discovered that, even if he didn't have to rely on me when he needed to fuck, he'd rather do so, and I had no objection to lending myself for that purpose. He'd got over the danger of falling in love with me, or so I imagined; and surely there was no likelihood I'd fall in love with him. Was there? Anyway . . . I was going home to England in a fortnight.

The de los Rioses said they would buy the Smrkovskys a new swimming pool and pay for their garden to be re-landscaped. This appeased the Smrkovskys, so lawyers were kept out of the matter, which was wise. Kim was *not* asked to do the work. Katya had now finished summer school, so she and I began to enjoy ourselves; days on the beach, walking in the hills, dinner parties.

When Kim and I had sex it was in the afternoons. It

isn't always the man I screw with, I said to myself, whom I want to sleep with. The man who wraps his arms round me at night, whom I trust enough to breathe against from midnight till dawn, isn't there just for sex. Who is he and where is he? I don't know. I don't think it's Kim.

« TWO »

Do you get more pleasure from sex," I asked, "if it happens spontaneously, like if I say 'Let's have it now' and we do, or when you know we will in, say, twelve hours' time, and you're looking forward to it all day?"

"There isn't any difference." I'd hoped Kim's reply would be 'Let's have it now' but his thoughts were not on me. He was staring up at the mountain-top above the monastery. It was on fire.

"I think there's more pleasure when it's spontaneous," I said. "Sometimes, if I've got . . . uh . . . an appointment in the evening, I have butterflies of nervous excitement. So when I get into bed I'm tense . . . which doesn't help."

"I'm always getting a hard for no reason at all."

"That's because you're twenty-one. I'm forty."

"Oh." He continued to stare at the smoke billowing up into the sky.

He'd called in to ask if Katya still wanted the hedge

trimmed; she'd said something, the previous week, about needing to get it done. There might not be any point right now, she answered a little sadly. To take their minds off things, I said, "The worst example of sexism I've seen for years is in this morning's paper."

"Is that right?" Katya said. She, too, was looking out of the kitchen window.

"It says Isabelita Peron was on holiday last month in Sitges. The reporter happened to see her wearing a low-cut bikini, so he wrote: 'Who would have thought this busty lady was once President of Argentina?' "

"What's sexist about that?" Kim asked. Katya was obviously not listening.

"Can you imagine anyone would ever say of Juan Peron 'Who would have thought this well-hung man was once President of Argentina?' "

"What?" Katya asked.

"I don't understand," Kim said.

"I give up!" I did.

"I hope the wind changes," Katya said, for the tenth time.

The fire had been burning for three days. It had started on the other side of the mountain, near the reservoir, and already a huge area was a blackened desert. The casualties were hundreds of trees, bushes, wild flowers, some animals, and twenty houses. The occupants of the houses had escaped in good time. Arson, it was rumoured; but no one could be sure: the weather conditions were such that an inferno could blaze from a carelessly discarded cigarette end, could even develop from purely natural causes. The summer had been unusually hot; the land was tinder dry; strong, almost gale-force winds were blowing in each day off the Pacific and over the Santa Cruz Pass. If the mountain-top became well alight the wind could fan the fire down the Los Gatos side, and Katya's house would be right in its way. Her road ended in the grounds of the monastery a quarter of a mile up the hill; beyond that were vast acres of forest, dry as a bone.

My twitterings about sex and the Perons were attempts to stop Katya and Kim thinking the unthinkable: the destruction of the houses and gardens of Los Gatos. And also because I felt I had a guilty conscience to salve, though there was no good reason to feel guilty: on Thursday I was flying back to England. The plane ticket had been booked months ago and it couldn't be altered. I was a rat leaving a sinking ship, abandoning my best friend and my lover of that summer when they needed me most; and there was nothing I could do about it.

A sinking ship: the wild life of the mountains was already taking precautions. First, the birds: all morning they had been in flight, winging away from the flames towards the town, a direction in which they never flew. Then animals that were rarely seen in the gardens—gophers, and a couple of raccoons—hurried across the lawn. Katya, observing them, said, "We don't want a bunch of rattlesnakes to visit."

"Rattlesnakes!" I echoed.

"You get them in the hills. They're very shy, but you can hear them in the undergrowth. Their water-holes dry up by September or October, so they venture near the

houses then. People see them in their gardens on swelter-
ing hot nights."

"Ugh!" I shuddered.

"Well . . . with this . . . "

Next day Kim and I walked through the monastery grounds,
towards the flames. He was exhausted. Yesterday he'd
volunteered as a fire-fighter and had done a seven-hour
shift in addition to his usual gardening work. He'd had
almost no sleep. He smelled, even though he had showered, of wood smoke and ashes, and his eyes were red and
sore. The sweat-band he was always wearing round his
blond locks was cratered with little black burn-holes. He
was returning to another fire-fighting stint, and was trying
to persuade me *not* to join in too.

"It isn't your fire," he said. "You're leaving the day
after tomorrow."

"So what? Any help is surely welcome!"

"I think you should be with Katya." That thought
had crossed my mind. "I guess they'll have to evacuate
the town . . . at least those houses nearest the fire,
which include hers. She could need you to help pack
things, and . . . she's alone."

No sign of the monks: they were, presumably, fight-
ing the blaze or beginning to move their possessions out. I
looked at the vines, peach trees, olives, all heavy with fruit.
Beyond, further up the mountain, eucalyptuses and oaks.
Fennel, escallonia, blackberry, withered grass. Limp dry
leaves. Marigolds in bloom. Insects, unaware of anything

out of the ordinary, busy on insect business. Dust. Dust, dust and ash. Ash hovered in the shafts of sunlight, which were not the gold slanting columns they should have been at this time of year but pale yellow, filtered through smoke. The smoke made us cough. Up at the summit flames crackled, and the smoke lifted thousands of feet into the air. A party of fire-fighters, their turn finished, trudged down the mountain: dejected, grimy, so weary they were almost asleep on their feet. I pulled Kim off the trail, and led him to a tree against which I leaned. "What is it?" he asked.

Although more fire-fighters were visible, coming alone or in pairs down from the summit, I put my arms around him and kissed him tenderly. "I'll go back to Katya," I said.

"That's the best kiss you've ever given me." His voice was quietly amazed.

I was beginning to see him as a man with qualities, not just a hunk of flesh with an efficient cock. I smiled, ruefully. "It's a bit late, isn't it! Too late, I guess."

"Is anything ever too late?"

I didn't reply.

He said: "You know . . . I've just been a sex machine . . . because that's what you wanted. But I do have feelings. Especially for you."

We kissed again. Stroked each other's skin. "I hope that erection is a bit less obvious when you reach the fire," I said. "I wouldn't like it charred to a crisp."

"David . . . I love you." He looked astonished, and very embarrassed, by what he'd said; he broke away from me and hurried off, up the mountain. I watched him till he was out of sight, distress falling over itself inside me, like tumbling clothes in a dryer.

The wind did not drop, and rain was unheard of in September, unless a freak storm drifted up from Mexico. The fire-fighters couldn't hold the blaze; it crossed the summit and burned huge boulevards down through the trees: in forty-eight hours it would reach the first houses of Los Gatos. The police warned people to pack essential possessions and be ready to abandon their homes at a moment's notice.

"I'm not leaving these," Katya said, as she piled her precious collection of Russian literature into tea chests. Tolstoy, Pushkin, Dostoevsky, and Gogol lay in untidy heaps. First editions of Pasternak and Chekhov, bought by her grandparents in Tsarist Russia, lay scattered on a floor half the world, and in an utterly different civilization, from their place of origin. It would be an appalling crime if they were destroyed. Yet, I thought, the loss of the monks' fruit trees, and the whole mountainside that had given me such pleasure, would be no less horrifying. Some of my history would be vanishing in flames.

"Where will you go?" I asked.

"To Berkeley. I've friends there. Many old friends."

"I wonder about Kim."

"His parents moved to Hawaii soon after he started to work in the gardens. I said he can come with me."

"That's kind of you."

"He's . . . O.K. More to him than I'd thought."

"I'd reached the same conclusion," I said. And smiled.

She laughed, not unsympathetically. "Life seems to be conclusions," she said. "Most of them reached too late." She picked up her copy of *The Cherry Orchard*. "Chekhov knew all about that, more than anyone. 'Mamma asks you not to cut the orchard down until she's left.' " She sighed, lost for a moment in the past. "Tell him to come to England. Or . . . if not that . . . sleep with him tonight."

"I will," I said. "Maybe both."

"I should find the cat before he gets himself burned to a frazzle." She went to the window and called, "Redford! Robert Redford! Come to Mamma!" But Redford didn't appear. We found him, later, asleep in the garage.

By early evening everything was packed. My possessions went quickly into one suitcase, so I went down to the cottage and fetched Kim's clothes and his few personal belongings. Katya's trunks, bags, and tea chests were in the hall—books, records, clothes, ornaments, and souvenirs from various parts of the world. Most of the stuff in the house was not hers. The furniture, carpets, drapes, even the crockery and cutlery were the owner's, and he lived in Japan. There was not much we could do about this, we decided; even if we did pack it all we wouldn't know where to take it.

There was no need to flee at once. It was unlikely, we thought, that the fire would get to us till tomorrow morning at the earliest; its progress in our direction, though inexorable, was not rapid. The disused school near the summit was well alight, and the trees and bushes near it that I knew and loved would undoubtedly be in flames. The sky was overcast, not with cloud, but with acrid smoke, worse than a dense Los Angeles smog. It was impossible to find anywhere, indoors or out, that did not reek of burning. Our throats were sore, and we couldn't stop coughing. Our neighbours were packed and ready too, so it was peculiar that none of us got into our cars and drove away.

"Because we can't believe it," Katya said. "To get out now . . . it means we really do think the place will be burned down. No . . . we'll hang on till the last possible minute. But I must say . . . if the Smrkovskys and the de los Rioses go, I'll get very nervous."

"We have to wait till Kim is back," I said.

"Oh sure! I wasn't thinking of right now or even tonight, but . . . maybe . . . noon tomorrow."

"We could put everything into the cars."

There were two cars—Katya's Peugeot estate waggon, which we'd often grumbled about because it was ancient and quite unnecessarily big, and Kim's Oldsmobile, a prehistoric, battered and even more unreliable chariot, which was kept on the de los Rioses' drive. We just about managed to get everything into both, with a few inches of space for one passenger (me) and the two drivers. I would have to have Redford, in his box, on my lap: he wasn't in it yet, of course, but he was now confined to the house, which annoyed him considerably.

When we had finished, Katya said, "Just because

everything's going up in flames doesn't mean we should deprive ourselves of a drink. It's *long* past the cocktail hour, and there's a full bottle in the kitchen cupboard."

We were on our second vodka when Kim arrived. He was dead beat: his face smudged, his clothes singed, and his hair almost black. He put his arms round me and kissed me, then lay full-length on the couch and shut his eyes. I went over and knelt by him. "I love you," I whispered.

He smiled, felt for my hand, and said, "But you don't mean it." Before I could answer he was asleep, and snoring.

"*Do* you mean it?" Katya asked. I didn't think she'd heard.

I extricated my hand, walked across the room, looked out of the window, picked up my drink, and lit a cigarette. Then said: "I guess not."

"Was it wise, then?"

"I . . . I didn't totally not mean it." I glanced at my watch. "This time tomorrow . . . I'll be on a plane, over a thousand miles away from here. Quite possibly he and I . . . will never see each other again. But I think he needed to hear it."

She nodded. She understood. She said: "The consequences of actions."

"I know one never knows them at the time."

She swirled the ice cubes in her drink. "The first man I ever went to bed with . . . I did so out of politeness. To say no seemed dreadfully rude! I was seventeen." She laughed. "And the first time I ever said 'I love you'—no it wasn't the same man! Good God!—I didn't mean it. I lived to regret that. I said it because . . . it was expected. When you're young you don't want to disappoint."

"But you learn that it's essential to disappoint. If you wish to go on being a sane, functioning, intact human."

"Sure."

"Youth is terrifyingly judgmental," I said. "It smashes its clay-footed idols with gusto."

"Again . . . sure."

"As I said . . . I didn't not mean it."

She grinned.

At midnight Kim woke and asked if he could take a shower. "Of course," Katya said, and he stumbled into the bathroom. Then Mr de los Rios and Mr Smrkovksy came to the front porch. It wasn't dark; the sky was reddish, glowing: the flames were clearly visible, now halfway down the mountain. We could hear the distant shouts of the fire-fighters. Mr de los Rios said he had just called the police, who told him they didn't think it necessary to get out tonight, but, should the situation change for the worse, they would come round and knock on people's doors. Katya was reassured when he and Mr Smrkovsky said they wouldn't leave without telling her they were doing so.

When we returned inside, Kim was out of the bathroom. Katya insisted he should have some food.

"I'm too tired," he said.

"When did you eat last?"

"Oh . . . this morning."

"Then I'll fix you some peanut butter sandwiches. And a vodka tonic."

"I'm not crazy about peanut butter sandwiches."

"It's all we've got left. Everything else is packed."

"Don't worry about it, then."

"Do as you're told!"

He submitted. When he had finished eating, she said to me: "Take him to bed." Kim was startled. "You can have my room," she went on. "The guest-room bed is much too monastic."

It was the first time we made love, as opposed to having sex. A far cry from the athletic fucking we'd always indulged in: sweet and tender; the emphasis on kissing and stroking of skin. He was gently licking my face when he came in my hand. I looked at the sperm on my fingers, and said, "I wish I could keep it. For ever." And I started to cry.

Mrs de los Rios knocked on our door at seven. They were leaving, she said, and so were the Smrkovskys.

There was no sunlight: what, in my sleepy state, I thought an unusually thick mist was smoke. A bush in the garden burst into flame. It took us five minutes to dress, put Redford in his box, and grab the last of our things (the sheets from the beds, and the glasses we'd been using). I sniffed the sheet: Kim and me mingled, and wood smoke. "Goodbye old house," I whispered. Katya locked the front door, and we went to the cars. I was driving with her. I kissed Kim, and said, "I'll see you in England."

His eyes lit up. "That would be great! Boy! But . . . I'd never raise the money."

"We'll work on it."

"Anyhow . . . I'll see you again this morning. At the airport."

I'd reckoned, when I left home on this vacation, that I'd be happy to get back, that I'd be looking forward to the return; I'd reached the age when a six-week absence from things familiar was quite enough. I was wrong. As I flew east images of Kim were an almost physical wound, and thoughts of Katya suddenly having to cope with the Berkeley she nowadays detested; the house and garden ablaze; the flowers, the monastery, the trees . . .

It was unexpectedly hot in London, and I and all my friends and acquaintances spent that first week-end I was back sunning ourselves in our gardens. I suppose I would normally have enjoyed the small change of the conversation, relating my adventures on the other side of the world, and listening to Maria and Dizzie telling me how they built their patio doors, the problems Maggie and Eve had encountered in buying their house, the concerts Chris had been to, Keith leaving Adam, the cute chicken Tony was sleeping with, the row between Martin and Rick at Keith's party. But ache for Kim, Katya, and burnt Los Gatos filled me entirely.

For a week or so we talked on the phone every day. The fire was now under control: the wind had dropped and fog had set in, or a kind of ashy smog, dark as a Victorian pea-souper; as murky, Katya said, as the opening pages of *Bleak House.* They'd been to Los Gatos to look at the destruction. The town itself had been saved, but nearly all the houses on the edge where Katya lived were gone, hers included, and the Smrkovskys' and the de los Rioses'. She refused to describe the scene; it would depress me unutterably, she said. Kim said he'd never spoken to anybody six thousand miles off, and, as if he didn't quite trust the telephone, he yelled so loudly each time that I had to hold the receiver about a yard away from my right ear.

"I miss you," I said.

"I miss you too." There was a long pause, then he said, "Katya's with me."

"Tell her to go outside."

I heard him say to her: "You're to go outside." She laughed, and a moment later he said, "She's out on the deck."

"I want your big huge arms round me. And kisses, and I want your furry gold skin to touch. I want to hear you breathe. I want your cock in me."

"Don't. I'll . . . just like you that last night . . . I'll cry." Another pause, very long this time. "Here's Katya."

They were settling down in Berkeley as best they could, she said. But it was strictly temporary. She was negotiating for a house in Menlo Park; she couldn't face living in Los Gatos: it would be too sad. She was pulling strings to get Kim a job, and he could rent a room in her house. (Katya excelled at pulling the right few strings.) We'd all meet up next summer, she said. In England.

"All?" I queried.

"Me, you. And Kim, if you want him."

"But how could he afford the flight? The spending money?"

"If I tell him you really want him to come . . . that in order to do so he'll have to earn sufficient cash, save it for the fare and so forth . . . he'll do it. He's got a lot of guts. And affection for you."

"I want him to come."

"Then it's a deal."

"You're a witch, Katya. A white goddess! Meanwhile . . . keep him off the streets."

She laughed. "I never interfere with other people's sex lives. You ought to know that!"

"I love you both."

It was a long time before I could bear to think of last days in Los Gatos, but this conversation lifted my spirits: a sense of guilt had been removed. Next summer I'd give them the best holiday they would ever have.

« THREE »

It was a rare example of absence genuinely making the heart grow fonder; to such an extent, I began to think, that if for some reason he was unable to come to England in July, it would then be an example of hope deferred making the heart very sick indeed. I needn't have worried. Every phone call, every letter, was a message of excited anticipation, though the letters were brief and the spelling . . . laborious. Putting words on paper didn't come as naturally to Kim as making love or digging gardens. I had a few doubts now and then: the callous attitude to the Smrkovskys' dog—could he be callous with me? But I was in love, in love for the first time in years; all the soft, tender emotions: plans for sharing, caring, for making him happy. Pipedreams, I told myself: he was merely coming for a summer holiday.

But a dancing bubbly phone call in November—Kim yelling so loudly the neighbours could have heard him—followed by a long, detailed letter from Katya was the best news of all. She had applied for, and been granted, secondment from the university for a whole year, and was going to spend it in London. Negotiating for this had taken several weeks, but, she explained, she'd said nothing about it to me before, because the chances of her application being successful had seemed to be so very slim. She wanted a year away from work to write a book on Chekhov, *the* definitive critical biography (a comment that was followed by three exclamation marks and four question marks). The powers-that-be at San Jose had pointed out, quite rightly, that she didn't have to go to London to do this, which was why she had thought they would turn her down. But they'd relented: Katya had given San Jose students nearly a quarter of a century of good teaching, and she'd never previously asked for a sabbatical. Would I therefore find a suitable apartment she could rent from mid-July onwards, not too many subway stops from the British Museum and, as she put it, "Downtown London". Somewhere between there and my house in Stoke Newington would be ideal, she said. Kim, of course, would be coming with her for the entire year, if I could help him financially. He wouldn't be able to earn his living in England; the British authorities would be unlikely to allow an inexperienced gardener to have a work permit. Maybe I could find him a pub job that was paid out of the petty cash, or ask my friends did they want their trees cut down. (On second thought, she said, probably *not* the latter.) She assumed Kim would be living with me, so she only wanted a small flat—a studio with bathroom and kitchen would do.

There was a postscript in Kim's handwriting. "A whole year with you. Every night in your bed. I can't *wait!*"

Colleagues at work (I taught at Queen Charlotte) noticed my effervescent mood during the next few weeks, and said I must be in love—though not all of them realised the person in question was another man. Even some of my students remarked on the change; I was at last making eminent Victorians seem like a pleasure, one of them said. Friends, of course, knew more of the details, and hoped—at times with doubtful voices—that it would turn out to be precisely what I wanted. Martin said, enigmatically, "I suppose you'll find your pants when the rainbow ends," and Chris said, "If people get their hearts' desire, they have to learn how to live with it." But Tony told me to "Go for it, you jammy sod"; Maria and Dizzie thought it quite wonderful, just like Barbara Cartland, but much better of course; and Keith said he wanted a man to mow his lawn and prune his roses, even if he was ugly, which, knowing my taste, Kim probably was.

Finding Katya somewhere to live might be difficult, I thought, but it wasn't. I said to myself: my luck can't go wrong. A lecturer at Queen Charlotte was going to India for the whole of the next academic year, and wanted someone to live in his basement flat in Alameda Street, Islington. It was bigger than Katya had asked for, but the rent was not exorbitant, and it had a garden. We settled the deal in five minutes. So . . . roll on the next academic year! The only problem was that the present one was a real drag. Time went as slowly for me as it had done in boring classes at school when I was a teenager.

In love I was, but it wasn't my nature, the object of
my desires and affections being a whole continent, an
ocean, and many more months away, to be a complete
sexual hermit. Not that I had any inclination towards
promiscuity: AIDS ruled that out, and, being forty, I
wasn't so anxious as years ago to score with a different
guy every Saturday evening. But I did meet a man one
night at the Hippodrome, another blond, though not at all
like Kim; slighter in build, pale, with straw-coloured
hair. Sex, in his flat in Muswell Hill, was the other way
round. Good, though, and we continued to meet occasionally, for a meal or a film, or dancing at a disco, and a
night in bed. I said from the start I was very much involved with somebody else. That was perfectly O.K.,
Mike answered. He had two other lovers he saw regularly,
Robert and Paul; he wasn't, at this time of his life, looking for commitments. He was thirty-one, and had recently
broken up with a man he had lived with for ten years. A
nasty, messy break-up. He was not yet ready, he said, for
another deep relationship, though he thought it was what
he would want one day.

He was a pleasant, easy-going person, with a nice
sense of humour; an intellectual who wrote poetry, and
some of his work had been published. He, too, was a
teacher—of French, at a large comprehensive school in
North London. If our circumstances had been different, I
thought at times, if we had both been looking for a relationship, something good, even long-lasting, might have
developed between us. We had a great deal in common;
whereas Kim and I had nothing, apart from a little shared

history, the benevolence of Katya, and a love of each other's bodies that bordered on worship.

I was worried, at first, about sex with Mike: AIDS. But I was reassured when he said Robert and Paul had no other partners. They, too, were worried about AIDS, and were content, albeit reluctantly, only to sleep with him. Fine—except for wondering who Paul and Robert had been with before they met Mike. But anyone I'd been fucking, or who'd fucked me, in the years immediately before I met Kim was also a risk; total safety was not to do it at all. Nothing and nobody was really safe now: at least the present situation was less dangerous than some I could have found myself in.

I told Kim, in a long phone call in January, about Mike, and he didn't seem to object. We had agreed we shouldn't demand a monastic twelve months; we were sufficiently confident of our feelings for extra-marital sex not to matter. When he arrived in England, I said, I wouldn't see Mike again, unless it was simply on a friendship basis. "What about you?" I asked. "I don't suppose you've been totally celibate."

"Not exactly," he answered.

"Tell me."

"I've been . . . cultivating my twenty-five per cent."

"I don't understand."

"A woman. Well . . . it's less chancy; that's for sure."

"A woman!" I was surprised. I'd almost forgotten that Kim, strictly speaking, was bisexual, though I now remembered a dream he'd woken from on our last morn-

ing in Los Gatos. He'd mentioned it, as I watched the
bush burning in the garden, and heard Mrs de los Rios
saying to Katya that they and the Smrkovskys were leaving. He'd been making love to Loretta Lynn, and her va-
gina afterwards was full of rose petals. It was a beautiful
dream, he said. "Do I know this woman?" I asked.

"Yes."

"Oh?"

He hesitated. "I haven't told you before
. . . because I figured it might bother you."

"Why should it?"

"Because . . . it's Katya."

To say I was astonished would be far too mild; a
cliché like hit in the solar plexus would be nearer the
truth. "But . . . but she's fifty!" was my first—rather
daft—reaction.

"I like older people. You're forty."

"Yes . . . yes, but . . . "

"You *are* bothered."

"I don't know. I don't know . . . what to think."

"We were lonely. That's all. Listen . . . I love you.
You and just you. I can't wait for the time we kiss, and
hold each other, and say . . . all the things I want to say,
and hear you say. Silly things, private things. Beautiful
things. I . . . I adore you, you lovely man."

I took a deep breath, and tried to pull myself together. "I want that too," I said. "I can't wait, either. I love
you. It's all right." Then, after a pause, "Have you been
doing it often?"

"Not as often as you and I do it."

I had a bad moment suppressing jealousy, but realised he could have felt the same when I was talking about Mike. "She never even hinted at it in her letters," I said.

"We . . . discussed that. I said *I* wanted to tell you. *Had* to tell you; if it came from her, you'd think me a coward. Or involved, or some such bunch of shit. Listen . . . we all need sex. And somebody in your bed is better than nobody."

"I can understand that all right."

"I love you."

"You're sure you'll be living with me, and not with her when you get to England?"

He laughed. "I told you . . . every night!"

"Come *soon.*"

"Five months and twenty-three days. We touch down at London Heathrow on July thirteen at ten after ten in the morning. You'd better be there!"

"I'll *certainly* be there!"

I tried hard to come to terms with this piece of news, but I wasn't totally successful. I was being illogical and immature, I reasoned; it was much better, safer—that it had been a woman, and it was less of a threat also. But if Kim had fucked a casual male pick-up, and because of the AIDS scare had used a condom, I'd have thought nothing of it. The attitudes to gay life I'd absorbed in the past twenty years had led me to believe that screwing around in a lover's absence was harmless, indeed could be beneficial. AIDS had inevitably changed that, but I hadn't changed in my moral stance. So, why should I object to Kim and Katya?

Because it was my lover and my best friend. I felt, somehow, left out. I began to wonder, with the three of us soon to be together in England, if it would cause any really serious tensions. Katya had been in one slot in my life, Kim in another, separate, even though they were living in the same house. Now they had shifted into a slot of their own. I couldn't justify my feelings at all: but I did not like what had occurred.

Kim evidently told Katya of our conversation, for her next letter was an attempt to pour oil on waters she guessed were troubled. Her customary intuition was working well: "The first time it happened," she wrote, "it just *happened*. I can't explain why exactly, but, believe me, neither of us had made a play for each other, or been motivated by hours of unrequited lust. At the time of the event I don't know which of us was the more astonished. I'm not trying to steal him from you; I'm not in love with him, nor he with me. I'm fond of him of course, but I don't regard him as some divine being, physically, or as a person. I haven't altered my views on the limitations of his character: if I were to think of him as a real lover, I'm sure—forgive me for saying it—I'd get bored pretty rapidly. He told you we were lonely in our separate bedrooms; that's the truth, and no less than the truth. Of course I have to admit it's been enjoyable—sex with a good-looking, vigorous, uninhibited young man is obviously a pleasure, and I know you don't need me to tell you that! I guess you feel hurt—betrayed even—and I understand. You aren't my oldest friend, but you *are* my closest friend, and I'm not going to let anything

—certainly not Kim—spoil our relationship. If you say I shouldn't do it again, I won't. David, I promise. I've decided to postpone my trip to England by a couple of months. Kim will be there in mid-July as planned, so you two can have a while by yourselves to iron out any problems. I'll still pay the rent on the apartment from mid-July, as I don't want to lose it."

That reassured me a little, and I wrote back saying of course I didn't feel hurt, that she wasn't to be so silly as to pay for a flat she wouldn't be using till September, and to arrive with Kim in July. She answered: "I'll split the difference and come the second week in August. It gives you both a month without me, and I'm sure that's good."

I discussed these problems with Mike, one evening over a drink. "Ah!" he said. "It's the old syndrome. You can do as you please when your lover's away, but you get very cross if he does it too."

"I don't think it's at all like that." But it was, to some extent.

"I believe . . . that real love—passionate, romantic, sexual love—is one to one. You don't want anybody else. It's exclusive. If you're always having something on the side, and you stick together, it's for other reasons —friendship, security, shared interests."

"I suppose you're right. But as with all generalisations . . . only partly right. Anyway . . . *you* don't live like that."

"I did once."

"And how are your other two lovers?" I asked.

"I'm not seeing Paul just now. Well, I am seeing

him . . . but not for sex. He's got flu rather badly. Doesn't seem to be able to shake it off."

"Are you coming home with me?"

Mike looked amused. He finished his beer, and said, "Yes. Let's get on with it."

His head, when he came, always jerked and flopped against my shoulders. His trademark, so to speak. I liked that.

He lay on his back, blowing smoke rings at the ceiling. "When Kim is here . . . I imagine you won't be wanting us to do this."

"It . . . could be . . . difficult."

He ground out his cigarette. "That's what I thought."

"Does it bother you?"

"Yes and no. You see . . . I *like* you. I'll miss *you* . . . as much as *it*."

I didn't answer. I felt uncomfortable, and ashamed.

"Maybe," he said, "when he's gone back to America . . . we'll get together again. If I'm still around."

"Why shouldn't you be?"

"Oh, I could have run off with Mr Right. Anyway . . . I guess we can meet socially when Kim is here. No harm in that, is there?" He snuggled down under the duvet. "Let's sleep now. I'm tired."

I was thinking about all these things next day, during my shiatsu session. Shiatsu is Japanese for "finger pressure," and it's like acupuncture without needles;

Danny, a young student of mine last year, now a qualified teacher who couldn't get a job, had taken it up in a big way. He wanted to qualify as a shiatsu expert, and, needing people to practise on, had roped me in. I went once a week, and enjoyed it; it made me so relaxed I often fell asleep while he was working on me. He had had an affair with a lecturer from our Drama department, but it had ended not long ago. He was cute, particularly in the white karate-style clothes he wore for our sessions. When our eyes met on these occasions, he would grin, mischievously. I liked his eyes. His touch, too, which was warm, confident, and gentle. Today, as he maneuvered my left leg, my toes brushed against his cock. It was very hard. I did not react to this at all, much as I would have liked to take him into bed; it would change our relationship, so that the shiatsu thereafter, I felt, would be valueless. I could store the moment away in my memory, I said to myself, for future reference, perhaps. Or just make an oblique comment about it: acknowledge it.

When he had finished, he said, "You're a bit far away this morning. And there are tensions in your neck."

"What does that mean?"

"You have something bothering you, maybe."

"Yes. I don't terribly like myself just now." He looked surprised, but said nothing. As he was clearly hoping I'd reveal more, I went on: "My lover is arriving from America in July. He's been sleeping with my best friend, and it upsets me. And I've told the man I've been sleeping with in his absence that we can't do so when Kim is here. I'm not happy I said that, either."

"I'd imagined . . . at your age . . . you'd have sorted out all that kind of stuff years ago."

"Nothing ever gets sorted out. That's one thing you learn with age."

"Interesting." He smiled, and his eyes twinkled.

"Does shiatsu usually loosen people's tongues?"

"Yes. Quite often."

"So . . . while I'm still in the confessional . . . my foot touched you. You were . . . "

He was, for a moment, extremely embarrassed, then he laughed. "I don't think, in the circumstances," he said, "not . . . with the entanglements you've been outlining . . . that I want to pursue that one. Not right now."

"I'm sorry," I said. "I shouldn't have mentioned it."

"It's perfectly O.K." He bent down and kissed me on the mouth. "I'll see you next Monday, at ten o'clock."

« FOUR »

He was disorientated, jet-lagged, bewildered—he'd been too excited to sleep on the plane, and it was four a.m. by his body clock when we arrived at my house—but he was overjoyed to see me. More beautiful than the mental image of him I'd kept the past twelve months: somehow my memory had diminished him; he was taller, broader, the frame and muscles bigger, the hair more golden, the skin more suntanned. He kept up a running commentary of child-like enthusiasm, during the journey from Heathrow, on everything he noticed—houses in pairs ("semi-detached," I said; he'd never heard of the word, nor entertained the concept) and made of brick! "Why don't you build in wood?" he asked.

"We don't have enough." He looked very puzzled.

"What's *that*?" He waved an arm at a pillar-box.

"What you call a mail-box."

"Gee! They're *red*! And cylindrical! They'd look cute in Los Gatos! Who's that man in the uniform and the comic opera helmet? A beef-eater?"

"A policeman."

"A British bobby! Wow! Now I know I'm in England!" He laughed delightedly, and slapped his leg. "God! This traffic! I thought that car was going to hit us, driving down the wrong side of the street."

"It's not the wrong side of the street. You're supposed to be on the left in this country."

"I couldn't deal with that," he said.

"You're born to it over here."

"What's that building with all the turrets and spires? St Paul's cathedral?"

"St Pancras Station."

"A *train* station? Oh, boy, that's neat!" And so on, all the way to Stoke Newington. In my living room he glanced round, and said, "I've never seen a house like this before. It's . . . *old*!" (Mid-Victorian, in fact.) Then he kissed me. "At least one thing's familiar," he said. "And it tastes better than I remember. You look better too! More . . . sexy." He kissed me again, one hand exploring the skin under my shirt till it found a nipple, the other unzipping my jeans. "Where's the bedroom?" he asked.

"Don't you want to freshen up after that long journey? Have something to eat?"

"Are you kidding? I want us with our clothes off."

Nothing jet-lagged here. "Stay in me!" I whispered, when we'd come; "Stay! You in me, throbbing, flexing, it's . . . *ecstatic*! Christ, how I *love* you!"

"You're not uncomfortable?" My legs were over his shoulders.

"No." I was aware of him gradually slackening, then, moments later, stiffening. A second coming, sticky, sweaty. And there might have been a third had he not fallen asleep, still in me, a dead weight in my arms. My face was buried in his hair; his breath moistened my cheek. I was very uncomfortable now, but I didn't move, even when pins and needles came.

During the weeks that followed I couldn't help but make contrasts with Mike. And others: the relationships of the past. No doubt about it—we were wildly unsuited. Would I, as Katya said of herself, get bored pretty rapidly? But what was rapidly? I was, at the moment, entranced; in love, and loving. There was nothing intellectual we shared, no tastes in common: books, the theatre, concerts, art galleries, were outside Kim's world. The cinema he enjoyed—not Truffaut or Fellini, but horror movies; and the more extraneous, sickening violence there was, the more he liked them. He didn't object to cathedrals and castles, though; they were "old", what he'd been told to look at and experience in Europe. So he preferred Westminster Abbey to St Paul's, because the tombs of Elizabeth the First and Mary Queen of Scots had been there nearly a century before Wren finished his masterpiece; and he'd heard of the two rival queens in high school history lessons, whereas Sir Christopher was as unknown to him as Frank Lloyd Wright or Edwin Lutyens. The Tower thrilled him, and the ceremonial outside Buckingham Palace ("Bucking-haamm" he pronounced it), but the ground where the National Theatre was he said could have been better used as a parking garage. The gay pubs he was not much interested in, but he loved the discos; the Hippodrome and Heaven, he thought were bigger and livelier than any in San Francisco, more full of "zap". He went down well with my gay friends. The women, Dizzie and Maria in particular, found him "sweet", and the men, sensing how physical it was between us, told me to get as much of it as I could while it was there. I found myself invited to many more parties now Kim was with me than I usually did: he was certainly decorative—and too innocent to notice the lust and envy he inspired, which made him all the more attractive both to me and the rest of the world. It's very good for morale to be with a man simply everyone wants to haul into bed, but who only has eyes for you. I often said to myself, I don't believe my luck; and . . . would it last?

"I can't compete with *that!*" said Mike, whom we met by accident, one evening at the London Apprentice.

It was a marriage of true bodies. Which seemed enough, quite enough, as a recipe for being content, safe, secure, and fulfilled. At my age I ought to have known better.

His enthusiasm, of course, was as endearing as his naivety. Teachers, outside the classroom it's said, never stop teaching, and I enormously enjoyed that role: points of language ("queue" for "line", "lorry" for "truck", that a fag was a cigarette, and that keeping one's pecker up wasn't a synonym for staying hard); the history of London's tourist attractions; looking to the *right* before you crossed a busy street; converting pounds into dollars; convincing him that a good restaurant in London wasn't a freak abnormality and that the fine, hot weather we were enjoying (he'd expected daily fog and chilliness, like a San Francisco summer) wasn't unusual in July and August.

"Gee, it's a great city! Am I glad to be here!" he said, over and over again, as he stared at Nelson's Column, drank a pint of bitter, rode on the top of a double-decker bus, observed city gents in pinstripes and bowlers ("Are they butlers?" he asked), or even when he bought a stamp to stick on a postcard to his parents in Honolulu— the fact that our stamps had the Queen's profile instead of a name to identify their country of origin, he thought "very British", full of "class", the correct "tone". There were some disappointments, of course. The price of tobacco and gas (petrol) was "through the roof", and his verdict on our supermarkets was "Hicksville". Having to put your groceries in bags at the check-out rather than a "store clerk" doing it for you, and the girl not saying "Have a nice day", was a reminder, he said, that Britain was on the decline, that our economy was third-world, and our influence minimal. (Many of the clichés about the United Kingdom, beloved by Americans, he decided were true, however much I pointed to evidence that illustrated the opposite.)

He certainly adored London, but his greatest admiration and excitement was for the country surrounding it. We drove into Surrey, Sussex, Hampshire and Wiltshire, stayed in a gay hotel in Brighton, and visited Stonehenge —the one curiosity more than any other all Americans long to see. The landscape was so beautiful, he said, so compact, so *green*. Sheep fascinated him—they were a

very rare sight in California. "You have trillions of them!"
he said, in amazement. And swans—"I've only seen
those birds in a zoo!" Thatched houses and pubs were a
marvel, a miracle. He would touch their whitewashed
walls, and say, "Adobe. It's unbelievable." Brighton impressed him, particularly the Pavilion and the gay life,
but Stonehenge was, of course, the biggest hit. He spent
ages strolling round it, absorbing it, photographing it.
"Three thousand years old!" he said. "Incredible!" The
only let-down was he could not go up to the stones and
touch them. "Wouldn't they look great on Twin Peaks!"
he said. "Then we'd have something worth talking about!"

"But you have," I answered. "The Golden Gate
Bridge. Alcatraz. Superb views and the most beautiful
houses in the world. Chinatown. Cable cars. The list is
endless."

"That's all a load of crap." (Like British supermarkets? I said to myself.) "I don't know what people see
in the Golden Gate Bridge. It's just a bridge, like dozens
of others. It isn't even golden!"

"It's where it is and what it stands for. Symbolism."

"What?"

Language problems again. Not the easy ones, phrases
of British English that could be translated immediately,
but the words that pointed to differences of education, experience, intellect, thought processes. "Symbolism," I
repeated. Explaining would make him feel I was showing
up his ignorance.

"I know what a symbol is," he said. "Well . . . I
think I do. But I don't see how the fuck the Golden Gate

Bridge is a symbol."

"It just gets to foreigners, maybe. To you it's ordinary. I'm not all that excited about these prehistoric stones, though their age is, yes, astonishing. The Golden Gate . . . it's California! It . . . sums it up! Freedom, the Far West . . . everything good about the place!"

"Oh." He shook his head, still puzzled.

There were several maladroit conversations of this sort.

But serene, pleasant nights at home, too, watching television, making love, doing domestic chores. It quickly became impossible to imagine the house without his presence: he fitted in so well it seemed he had always been there. I refused to contemplate what it would be like in a year's time when he'd gone, and we discussed, more than once, whether he'd one day want to be there permanently, and how that might be organized: could he just get "lost", or perhaps marry a British woman? He didn't see any good reason why he shouldn't want to settle in England. I earned enough to support us both, and he could always find a gardening job from someone who wouldn't say anything about a work permit. Daydreams!

Katya arrived, saw what the situation was, and said that, until my term started in October, she'd be busy at the British Museum and other libraries researching into Chekhov, but she hoped she'd see us from time to time in the evenings. She obviously didn't want to intrude too much on our privacy, and she declined my offers to take her round London; she'd done it all before, over and over, she said. But we met, the three of us, several times a week, for dinner, or a movie, or for drinks either at my house or at her flat—Alameda Street she quickly turned into a replica of her Los Gatos living quarters; books and papers and half-drunk cups of coffee and bottles of vodka were strewn on every available surface. She even found a black and white cat to substitute for Redford. (Redford too, was having a sabbatical—he was in San Jose, being looked after by a colleague of Katya's at the university.)

She seemed happy enough. I quickly forgot my fears about tension that might exist between us because she and Kim had slept together; neither of them behaved in any way like lovers, or ex-lovers. The subject was never referred to. She and I had had arguments before, a real ding-dong on one occasion when I'd demolished the rear bumper of her car when reversing my own, and she'd hassled me quite unnecessarily about the insurance claim; but we'd always made up our differences. The friendship was more important than any quarrel, and we were of an age not to bicker over a man; old friends were better than lovers, she'd said, when the Smrkovskys' dog had been killed.

What else could I want? It was Eden: my lover *and* my best friend, a cloudless August and September, vacation time, and a golden future ahead that would last a year, maybe more, maybe for the rest of my life . . . I remembered the scented, sweet nights in the gardens of Los Gatos, the question of Kim's I'd thought was as if I'd been offered the wrong kind of apple, and my answer—the quotation from *Kubla Khan*. It wasn't the wrong apple.

Weave a circle round him thrice,
And close your eyes with holy dread,
For he on honey-dew hath fed,
And drunk the milk of Paradise.

One morning the phone woke me. Kim was already up, and in the shower singing at the top of his voice —*Love, O careless love* . . . I threw off the duvet and ran downstairs to answer it. Mike.

"I've bad news," he said. "Very bad." He paused. "I've spent a week thinking about it before I could make myself tell you. Not this bit I'm going to say first, which I could have mentioned a month ago, but I didn't because I . . . I thought I shouldn't give you any unnecessary worries, what with Kim's arrival being imminent . . . Do you remember Paul had flu?"

"Yes."

"It wasn't flu. It's AIDS."

"Jesus Christ! How . . . how is he? Is he in hospital?"

"In St Anthony's having more tests, and he's doing pretty well. He's cheerful, and says he's determined to beat it, to survive . . . He can't, of course."

"Jesus Christ!"

"Listen . . . *my* bad news . . . I . . . mmm . . . decided I'd better take the test. I had the result last Thursday; I'm positive. No symptoms of anything, blood count normal, lymphocytes normal . . . and so on."

"Mike . . . oh, fuck! . . . I'm sorry. I'm sorry!"

"I had to tell you. And I must warn you: I may have passed it on to you. You have to make up your mind . . .

should you take the test as well. I'm going back to the hospital the day after tomorrow. Ring me before then, and let me know if you want to come with me." A long silence. "Are you . . . still there?"

"Yes. Mike . . . thank you for your honesty. It couldn't have been easy."

"Don't say a word about this to Kim. Not yet. You could be negative, and there's hardly any point in ruining it all for no purpose. And your friend, the one he slept with; what's her name?"

"Katya."

"Don't tell her, either. Not now. Promise me?"

"O.K."

"Can we . . . mmm . . . meet some time to discuss it?"

"Yes. I suppose so. I'll call you back."

"I'm sorry to . . . to hurl such a hand grenade. Very, very sorry."

I put the phone down. The September sun still streamed through the windows. My books were still in their right places on the shelves, the house-plants still green, an empty wine glass still where I'd left it last night on the mantelpiece. Mrs Brogan, three doors up, walked by; on her way to the shops, as was usual this hour of the morning. A blackbird sang in the garden. Dew was silver out there; it glistened on the grapes: my pride and joy, the grape vine that made a leafy roof over my patio. Kim was still singing his head off, the same song third time round, *Love, O careless love* . . .

My world had disintegrated. Just like that; in a five-minute phone call. Expulsion from Eden. The wrong apple: it had a maggot.

I trudged slowly up the stairs, into the bathroom. Kim, just out of the shower, was drying himself, steam rising in wisps from his skin. "Hey! What a nice surprise!" he said. "A male nude!"

He propelled me into the shower, and turned it on. "What are you doing?" I asked.

"We've never had it in running water before." He kneeled, and began to suck my cock.

"Don't. Not now. Please."

He looked up, startled. "Why not? You've *never* said no before. Never." I got hard, of course, and he was as upright as a flagpole. How could I stop him? I couldn't. Even if I hadn't promised Mike not to tell him, I couldn't say anything yet, not so immediately; the news so undigested, thoughts and feelings in a complete whirl . . . He screwed me, standing up in the shower, and after he'd come he sucked me off, while the hot water streamed down my hair and skin. He smiled, opened his mouth, and showed me. Then swallowed it. Honeydew. Milk of paradise.

"God! You made enough noise!" he said. "So I guess you liked it. But you don't look too happy."

"It was great." (I was aghast.) "Fantastic. Now let me dry myself, put my knickers on, and go downstairs and brew up some coffee."

"You have tensions in your neck again," Danny said.

(Kim was spending the afternoon with Katya.) "The past six weeks you've been so relaxed, and now . . . you're all knotted up. What's wrong?"

"A great deal. And this time I can't tell you."

"Oh?"

"Not now. One day, perhaps."

He continued with my neck, pushing hard on the pressure points, but after a while he grunted in disbelief, and gave up. He leaned over me, cradling my head in his hands. Five minutes of absolute stillness. Difficult to know what was in his mind, what vibrations he was receiving from me; but I felt immense comfort from his holding me like that: a baby with its mother. I wanted to cry.

"I'll work a little more on your stomach," he said. "All the lines of contact in the body meet there. The centre of things."

But the pressure on the abdominal muscles, on the bowels, and under my ribs, hurt; usually it soothed, made me sleepy. "It's no good today," I said.

"We'll stop. I'll make you some jasmine tea."

We drank this in silence. As I was leaving, he kissed me, as usual, on the mouth. I felt his tongue touch mine. Had that warm caring moment given him the virus too, I asked myself as I drove to Alameda Street. No. According to a Body Positive publication on AIDS—I'd had a copy of this for some while; yesterday, when Kim was in the garden, I'd taken it out of my desk and re-read it—kissing was unlikely to spread the disease: if it did, the number of victims would by now be astronomical. A shame I couldn't talk to Danny. I hadn't talked to anyone. It was incredible I hadn't told Katya, she who knew everything about me, my one confidante, my soul-mate! Give me time, I said to myself, give me time; I'll take the test, and if I'm positive, I'll tell Kim first, then Katya. If I'm negative . . . Mike's news will be the one secret of my life I'll *never* reveal.

But I had this dreadful certainty that my result would be positive.

« FIVE »

We tell all gay men they should have the test,"
Richards, the S.T.D. adviser said. I now know
how wrong he was. Amazing, when I think of it, that he
made no enquiry about my sex life—whether I was sleeping around, or in a one-to-one relationship—and did not
ask me if I'd informed my lover of my fears; never pointed
out what huge psychological damage could be caused by
being positive.

I suppose he had no knowledge of the catastrophes
that could occur in relationships, friendships, employment, housing—there had even been suicides—when the
results were positive. But he should have known: it
wasn't early days in HIV testing. He should have had
some inkling at least. Gone, certainly in most hospitals,
is the air of moral disapproval a gay man used to experience when he asked for a check-up, the feeling that if
you'd caught the pox it was your own fault for being a sex-
mad faggot; but there is still a belief that *all* gay men are

promiscuous: and that a disease is more interesting than the person who's got it, can somehow be isolated and looked at out of its human, social context.

Richards talked a great deal about "shagging"—a rather old-fashioned word I thought—and never once used an expression like "making love". It was as if he assumed I had no lover, just picked up men for a quick poke. He was convinced that the test was useful—that it would stop the spread of AIDS because all those gay men with a positive result would in future only screw with each other. He seemed to ignore the multitude of factors that lead to our taking a man into our beds—do we like him, for instance; nor did he have anything to say on the subject of how or when or where you told a prospective partner you were positive, or even if you could do so at all without that person fleeing in horror.

But, ignorant of these considerations, I took the test. Two tests; the second sample of blood was to see if my immune system was in any way damaged: unnecessary, of course, if I turned out to be negative—so the assumption already appeared to be that I was positive. I had a curious and not very pleasant feeling, while my blood was flowing into the phials, that I was important, rare, and very dangerous. Marion, the doctor in charge, wore gloves and a mask, and seemed to be nervous. The notes he had written about me and the phials were stamped "High Risk". He said afterwards, as he examined me for some of the obvious signs of AIDS, that a lymph node in my groin was slightly swollen—a very unhelpful comment, as lymph nodes can swell when any infection is present in the body, or for no reason at all. I left the hospital feeling unclean, contaminated, and asking myself how long did I have to live; were my insurances in order and where had I put my will—was it with my solicitor, or in my desk at home?

Mike had come to the hospital with me. We sat in a pub afterwards, and drank several glasses of wine. This man—my friend, and lover of a sort—may have given me AIDS, I said to myself. In which of our sessions in bed: the most exciting, or the least? As I came in him—that most normal and most satisfying of human pleasures—a lethal virus could have passed into my bloodstream through some minute, invisible abrasion in my cock. The irony of it: ecstasy and death were linked. It had often occured to me that orgasm and the moments after it destroyed, albeit briefly, the knowledge that one was mortal: I was like a god—fulfilled, rewarded, given point and purpose. It had not previously occurred to me that it could be the road to my own extinction.

I felt no anger against him, none at all. It was one of the risks any gay man took, nowadays. I'd known that risk and thought it minimal. There was no blame I could attach to Mike. I assumed that Kim, if he had to be told, would react as I did. This is an error most of us constantly make with our friends and lovers—we imagine, especially in times of crisis, that they'll perceive and reason as we do, that our moral codes are similar, that love and affection means we'll behave alike. If I thought at all, at this juncture, about what Kim would say or do should both of us be positive, I envisaged anger and hurt, but that such feelings would pass, and that the experience, however much he might freak out initially, would in the end bring us closer together. I could see no alternative.

I was surprised to find, after the shock had lessened, that I wasn't freaking out in any way. Despite thoughts of wills and insurance policies, I was more concerned with what I was going to cook when Katya came to dinner on Thursday, the holiday in the Westcountry Kim and I had planned, and the start of the autumn term in October. It's the only way to cope, I said to myself: get on and do whatever is next.

The dinner party was fine, and the week in Cornwall—helped by the apparently endless Indian summer—superb. Not so fine and superb as it would have been had the worry of the test result absented itself from my thoughts: it was due the day after we returned to London. I felt I was continually playing a part, performing as if nothing could possibly be wrong with life. Kim was enjoying his exploration of a new bit of the world too much to notice any change in me: I was a good actor, I decided. Most gays are, in my opinion; the years before coming out—being in closets and living double lives—give us that ability. Kim was preoccupied with swimming, surfing, eating good meals, walking on Cornish hills and cliff-tops, and falling in love with "old" things—Elizabethan Cotehele, even Truro cathedral, just a century in age. In bed I feared I'd be at my most vulnerable. I couldn't alter the ways we had sex, not till I knew; he'd demand explanations. Anyway, if I had the virus, I'd have given it to him long before Mike's phone call; would fucking now, or swallowing sperm, make much difference?

"Are you all right?" he asked me, one evening. "Is something bothering you?"

I feigned great surprise. "Of course I'm all right! Why on earth should you imagine I'm not?"

"I just thought . . . recently . . . you haven't been as enthusiastic as you usually are."

"In bed, you mean?"

"Yes."

I laughed. "What total nonsense!"

"In that case . . . let's do it."

"Sure."

I was positive. The news came by *phone*. Incredible! Those S.T.D. people are *inhuman*, I said to myself. No counselling, no advice, not a word of regret. All they were interested in was their one little piece of information. To them I wasn't a person. Just a statistic.

I had to tell him: get it over with immediately, right now; not brood for days, bottling it up. If I did that, I *would* freak out. Share it, be gentle and compassionate with one another, soothe each other's pain.

Gentle and compassionate, soothing: it would not be. I was never allowed to come so near him again, emotionally. Anger, vindictiveness, desire for revenge dominated his feelings: the weeks and months that followed were a slow letting go of me, done, I often thought, by inflicting as much hurt as he possibly could. This wasn't, perhaps, deliberately planned, not all of it, and there were moments when he shifted in the opposite direction; but on the whole our relationship became a battleground, he trying to wound, me trying to salve. He fought to leave me, and I fought to hold him. He could, of course, have left at once for California, never to come back, but he had nowhere there to go to—Los Gatos was burned, and the house in Menlo Park let for a year to strangers. He had to stay in London: Katya was here, and he saw her as his only friend: mentor and saviour.

Carrying on as normal, doing whatever was the next thing to do, was impossible, he said; an absurd attitude to life considering what had happened. He had put all his eggs in one basket—me—and I'd dropped it, smashed them all. He even accused me of suspecting that I had the virus, and had deliberately said nothing about it to him in order to get him into my bed. I was a monster, a black beast who'd done this terrible thing to him. Such ideas were crazy, I replied, lunatic; but to myself I said the feelings behind them were understandable; it would pass. He didn't refuse to have sex with me, however. In fact we did it as frequently as ever, which was strange, as his thinking about AIDS was wild, hysterical and ridiculous—it was, to him, a modern Black Death, an automatic killer, totally contagious. Ignorance, of course. In bed he wouldn't suck my cock any longer, wouldn't even touch it. Wouldn't kiss me. All tenderness had gone. My arsehole was simply a space in which to leave his sperm as roughly as possible.

"Don't," I said, more than once. "Please don't!" It hurt, physically as well as emotionally, as did the savage way he twisted and bit my nipples.

"Why not?"

"I don't like it."

"You're not meant to like it. You're being punished."

"You see your cock as a weapon to cause me pain?"

"Yes. Now just keep still and let me come."

I did. And had to help myself to my own orgasm. I could have refused to allow him to treat me like that, I suppose; I could have fought back, issued ultimatums, say I'd throw him out of the house. Many possible courses of action. Perhaps my willingness to permit him to do as he wished increased the contempt he had for me; I don't know. All I could think of at the time was that this was righteous anger, and my role was to find room for it, so it could eventually extinguish itself. It didn't mean, I said to myself, that he didn't love me any more, didn't need me, desire me, like me. Sense would at last prevail.

He decided to take the test, and I went with him to the hospital. As luck would have it, it was his twenty-third birthday; "The worst birthday of my entire life!" he said to me, several times. My present to him that morning was a book of photographs of Victorian London; he'd given it a brief glance and thrown it down, not a word of thanks. The card I'd bought him he wouldn't put on the mantelpiece. I also gave him a box of chocolates, and he allowed me to eat one half of one chocolate, selected by him; he ate the other half first. This childish ritual was kept up for a week—I was given half a chocolate each day—until Katya came round one morning when I was at

Danny's, and they wolfed the rest of the box between them.

He had not been to a V.D. clinic before. "I haven't had any of the illnesses!" he said. "Not even a suspicion of a symptom! And—fuck it! I'm not coming now for one of the ordinary ones, the kind of thing a sexually active guy my age would come for. It's not *fair!*"

The same S.T.D. adviser, the same doctor. Pleasant, but firm. Again no suggestion that because we were one-to-one lovers it might do more harm than good to take the test; no realisation that, even if we were both infected, we wouldn't be spreading the disease to others. Did that adviser, that doctor, think gay *couples* spent their nights sleeping around? They did not think at all—beyond we now have a test; let's use it.

He hated the needle jabbing into his vein. I hated watching it, particularly as the whole business was more protracted than when I had it done; for some reason his blood obstinately declined to spurt into the phial, just leaked very slowly.

"I think I'm going to faint," he said, and grabbed for my hand. He held it not as a lover would, but as a frightened child.

He didn't faint. Afterwards, in the hospital corridor, he heaved a great sigh, and not caring who saw us, let me embrace him. We stood there for a moment, stock still: the first tenderness since I'd told him. The anger's subsiding, I thought. I've played it right. He let me kiss him, the first time in a week. You can't kiss in anger, I said to myself. Our tongues touched. "I love you," I said.

"It must be very difficult for you, if what I'm going

through is any indication. I'm sorry."

"I love you," I repeated. "It's till death do us part now, isn't it?"

"Don't talk about death."

"I'll do anything . . . *anything* . . . to get us back to where we were."

He broke away. "It's impossible," he said. "And it isn't till death do us part. I still love you . . . but not enough to live with you." There was a very long way to go yet, I realised; this was no reconciliation. But at least he'd said it must be difficult—the first sign of pity, and sympathy, for what HIV might be doing to *me*.

We went out to dinner with Katya that night; it was meant to be a birthday celebration. She had a present for him, a glass sherry decanter she'd found in an antique shop; his thanks were fulsome, almost gushing. I thought of the reception my present had received, then: what on earth is Kim—jock Kim—going to do with an Edwardian sherry decanter? I felt so depressed I could hardly eat my food.

"Something's wrong," Katya said, looking from one to the other of us. She smiled. "Not serious, I hope?"

I dropped my fork on the plate, splattering hollandaise sauce. I couldn't meet her eyes.

"There's a great deal wrong," Kim said. "He—"

"Not now!" I said, sharply.

But he wouldn't be deflected. He told her the whole story. I suppose it was more or less accurate, factually, but the emotional slant he gave it made me sound vile— the serpent: the snake from the gardens of Los Gatos.

"There is no way," she said, when Kim had finished, "no way *at all* that David would have deliberately,
knowingly, slept with you if he'd had the slightest idea.
Come on! It's . . . utterly ludicrous!" She stared at him
until he lowered his eyes, then she turned to me. "I'm
. . . whatever can I say? . . . Sorry is absurdly inade-
quate. You must be in hell! Davy, Davy!" This diminutive
of my name she used only in moments of deep feeling; she
gripped my arm tightly, then leaned across the corner of
the table and kissed me full on the mouth, not once but
several times, as if to say *she* wasn't suffering from AIDS
phobia, wouldn't be throwing away a cup of hers I'd
drunk out of, or disinfecting the Alameda Street lavatory
pan after I'd shitted in it.

I pushed my plate away, the salmon almost untouched. I'd been unable to eat during Kim's recital,
and my dinner was now cold. I swallowed a glass of white
wine in one gulp. "Let's order another bottle," I said.

Katya empathised, had shown me fellow-feeling,
humanity, compassion. I felt almost astonished that
somebody could. Then, more sanely: well, why not? Everyone should be able to do so. Why should HIV positive
make me a leper? Why should a leper, anyway, be treated
as an outcast? We weren't living in the fourteenth century.

"I've been reading about AIDS," Katya said to
Kim. "Well, you can hardly avoid it; what's that appalling gutter newspaper they have here? *The Sun*, is it? It's
got even more garbage in it than *The National Enquirer*."
Kim never read newspapers: he looked puzzled. "You
know," she went on, "the one with the headlines like *I*

Had a Space Alien's Baby, or *Will Princess Di Get The Duchess of Windsor's Jewels?* and *Terrified Nurses Flee Deadly Gay Plague.* Not that I've been reading *The Sun* or *The National Enquirer.* Anyway . . . why are you so grossed out? As far as I can learn, AIDS is a very difficult disease to catch."

"Yes, that's just it!" Kim said. "It's like Russian roulette! Is it going to be *me*? Is it going to be *him*? Both of us? Neither? It isn't easy to get on with my life with *that* hanging over me!"

"You may be shot dead in the street by some maniac two minutes after leaving this restaurant. The food's excellent by the way. We must come here again." We were eating in Il Fàro in Camden Passage, five minutes' walk from her flat.

She was, momentarily, imagining London was dangerous, like an American conurbation. "I don't think you'll be slaughtered on the streets of Islington," I said.

"Well . . . knocked down by the Clapham omnibus." The mixed metaphor made me smile. She turned to Kim again. "Being HIV positive doesn't mean you'll automatically get AIDS," she said, "though battering your immune system with other diseases wouldn't help. Alcohol's also an immune depressant. And sperm. Do you have syphilis? Are you an alcoholic? How much sperm do *you* get up your ass?" He didn't answer. She went on, remorselessly: "The most likely trigger of all is stress, and Kim, you are lathering yourself up into a terrible load of it. Stop! Love him as you did before this happened. It's the only thing to do. Yes, take some precautions in bed.

Don't come into his mouth, and use a condom when you
fuck. Otherwise . . . carry on! What do you have to lose?
Just carry on!"

"You seem to know a great deal about it," I said. I
was surprised. "Have you joined the Terrence Higgins
Trust?"

She laughed. "No. I got bored with Chekhov today.
Did you know he studied medicine when he was a student? I
mean . . . I guess I'm not bored with Chekhov himself,
or his work. I just needed a change; I get tired of all those
gloomy Russians sitting around on padded settees and
saying, 'Isn't life *awful*? Have another drink.' When obviously their lives weren't awful at all, at least not the
middle-class bunch Chekhov knew. They could have
done all kinds of interesting things if only they'd bothered
to get their backsides in gear." She refilled the wine
glasses, and lit a cigarette. "I read something in the paper
about AIDS when I was having breakfast this morning,"
she said. "No, not *The Sun*! *The Guardian*. I was still
thinking about it when I arrived at the British Museum,
and I suddenly thought: fuck Chekhov. So I spent the
whole day reading everything I could get my hands on
about HIV, Kaposi's sarcoma, pneumocystis carinii, and
so forth. It helped to put those Russians in perspective.
Made me realise what an air-head Liubov Andreyevna
Ranevskaya was, and that Chekhov *meant* her to be."

"It's all very well," Kim said. "I just can't get it out
of my mind that David"—he pointed at me—"is dis-
eased. May have made me so. Or may not have made me
so, but he still could."

I was about to reply very angrily, but Katya waved an arm at me—an order to be silent. She looked at Kim, not with the contempt I'd expected, but sadly and seriously. She cupped her chin in her hands, put her elbows on the table. "Is that *all* you can see him as? Isn't he too a beautiful and special human being? A great friend? With a fine academic mind, a warm, generous, sympathetic personality, a lovely sense of fun? Has he ever deliberately done anything to hurt you? Isn't he a fantastic lay? You told me he was. Hasn't he cared for you, paid for you, given you his heart and head and body? Not to mention his house and his cheque-book. And you can only see him as a bag of viruses. You ought to be ashamed of yourself."

"I can't help it," Kim said. "I try. I really do try! But I'm shit scared. Shit, fucking *scared!*"

"I think you're a no-risk-taker."

"I took a risk! See where it's got me!"

"Going to bed with somebody is always a risk. Heavens, one of the consequences might be you have an orgasm! Help!! Crossing the street is a risk!"

"But AIDS is *not* one of the consequences."

Katya sighed, and looked at the menu. "Some birthday party this is," she said. "Let's get on to the dessert. I'll . . . have the zabaglione."

"So will I," I said.

"I am *scared*," Kim repeated. "I've read about AIDS too. Kaposi's sarcoma, the lot. The awful thing is . . . it's a death sentence, Katya! One year, two years, five years . . . and it kills you. And the death is horrible, slow, agonizing! I've read about people covered in skin cancers, gone blind, or who've got parasites in their brains, funguses in their throats and lungs. I don't want to die! Jesus, I'm *twenty-three*! What life have I had?"

"Or me, or David? We're all too young to die."

"You've both had a life. You're fifty. He's forty. You've done things. Been around. I've done nothing! And I want it *all*!"

"Are you having zabaglione?"

"What is it?"

"Yolks of egg, marsala and sugar, all whipped up and served hot with little macaroons."

"Sounds great."

"O.K. Zabaglione thrice." She summoned the waiter. "And three glasses of sambuca to go with it," she ordered. "They're on me, David." She returned to her argument with Kim. "I was born in 1936," she said, "in Moscow. Stalin's purges were at their height. Two months before I came into this world, my father was arrested on some trumped-up charge—he was never involved in politics, but he was the son of a minor government minister in Kerensky's administration—and sent to the gulag. I've never seen him. After two years' hard labour in a Siberian concentration camp he was shot. Or so we were told; my mother didn't believe it. He could still be in there for all I know. He was twenty-seven at the time of his arrest. What kind of a life do you think that was? Or—assuming he wasn't shot—still is?"

"I could be dead *before* I'm twenty-seven."

The zabaglione arrived. We ate in silence.

"Terrific," Katya said, wiping her mouth. "Let's count our blessings. Zabaglione is certainly one of them."

"How did you get out of Russia?" Kim asked.

"During the war, in the chaos that followed the German invasion. We were living in Viborg at the time, halfway between the Finnish frontier and Leningrad. It was in a part of Finland that had been annexed by the Russians in the Winter War of 1939. Anyway . . . the Finns decided they'd seize the opportunity to get their land back, as Russia was being scalped by the Nazis. So we were liberated. The soldiers were dressed in white, I remember; they looked like snowmen. My mother was half Finnish; she spoke the language. I was five years old. We stayed in Viborg—the Finns call it Viipuri—till 1943, then moved to Helsinki. In 1945 we went to America. To San Jose."

We drank coffee, then I asked for the bill. Fifty pounds, and my treat; my suggestion to come here: I'll pay, I'd said. And what have I had for my fifty pounds, I asked myself as I wrote out the cheque: a pretty dismal evening. A meal out, yes; but it hasn't cheered me up, not at all. Christ, I can do better things with fifty pounds!

"I need the bathroom," Kim said.

When he had gone, Katya said to me: "I'd diagnose him as a venerophobic."

"What's that?"

"Someone who has a morbid horror of venereal diseases."

"Katya . . . what am I going to do?"

She puffed on her cigarette. "Why don't you take him away on a trip somewhere?"

"My classes start next week."

"Be ill. Take him to Spain. Show him how much you love him. Pamper him. He'll come round. He has to . . . there being no alternative."

"Hmmm. I'll . . . work on it. Why Spain?"

"Spain, Schmain. Greece, Italy . . . where doesn't matter. He likes old things. Spain is practically rotting to bits, everything's so ancient. Well, that's what I'm told; I've never been myself." Perhaps I looked skeptical, for she leaned forward and kissed me. "It could work, you know, a vacation in Europe." It was as if she thought Britain not a part of that continent; the fifty-first state maybe? "Don't fight with him; listen to him; put up with his anger. In the end you won't regret a little perseverance; I'm sure of it."

"Sure you're sure?"

"Sure I'm sure I'm sure." We laughed; it was an old joke between us.

"You're a witch," I said. "You cast spells. I hope they're good ones."

We walked her back to Alameda Street. "You're coming in for vodka? Well, it goes without saying."

"Can I talk to you?" Kim asked.

We looked at him, surprised, then Katya said, "If you want. Do you mind, David?"

After a pause I said, "No."

"Shall I put him on the last bus?"

"Mmm . . . I'll leave you the car; you can drive him back. It's in Camden Passage. I'll get the bus."

Fifty pounds, and a ride home alone, on a bus too. A

night to remember? I guess not . . . but I remember it all too clearly.

I woke at three; he hadn't come in, but I slept again, not unduly bothered. Eight thirty: no Kim beside me. Now I *was* bothered. They've been fucking, I said to myself; that's what it was all about. "Talk to you alone." Huh! I'll kill him.

I rang Katya. "He's eating breakfast," she said. "Then I'm chucking him out. I want to be in the B.M. when it opens."

"My car is on a yellow line," I said.

"Christ! I forgot."

"Can you hurry up and get it? Another parking ticket! What . . . did you talk about?"

"He'll tell you, I'm sure."

"Anything I should know in advance?"

"Uh . . . I don't think so."

He didn't say very much; in fact seemed morose all day. Annoyed eventually by having every one of my questions deflected, I said, "I suppose the pair of you screwed. And you don't know how to tell me."

"That's about the gist of it," he replied.

The slap this was made me feel sick: a violent downward lurching in the stomach. "How . . . how could you!" I stormed. "When you might be positive! How could you *anyway!*"

"I used a rubber."

"When did you get that?"

"Last week."

"So . . . you've been thinking for a while you'd go to bed with her?"

"I might have been." He looked at me, very defensively. "Or I might have been thinking I'd use them with you. We will from now on, I guess."

"If you'd wanted to use them with me, you'd have asked me to buy some!" He didn't answer that. "Going to move in with her?"

"I told you . . . I love you. But not enough to live with you. Not now."

"What does she say?"

"About moving in? It came . . . as a surprise."

"And?"

"She's thinking about it."

"I don't believe this." I started to pace up and down the room. "I do not believe this is happening to me!" I realised I was shouting. "It's a nightmare, and I'm going to wake up in five minutes!"

"Calm yourself."

"How can I be calm!" I stopped by the table, and picked up a glass bowl I sometimes put flowers in. I wanted to crush it in my hands: if I couldn't hurt him, I wanted to hurt myself. Bleed. "Was the fucking good? Seventh heaven?"

"It's nice to lick cunt again." The attitude to the dead dog: not quite human.

I threw the bowl at him, as hard as I could: it smashed into his face. I didn't hang about to see if it sliced his beauty into blood-red ribbons, or merely hit him or knocked him over; I turned and rushed out into the hall. I heard glass splinter, then I dashed into the street, slamming the front door.

I walked and walked. Dazed. Shocked, stunned, trembling with hurt. Then . . . why did I do that? To *him*. *How* could I do it? I staggered into a telephone kiosk, and dialled Mike's number. "Can I come round? At once, right now?"

"Yes," he said. "I need to see you."

« SIX »

A wild wrestling; as if I was struggling to cheat mortality, to say no, no, I'll never die, I'm a god. He could sense the distress, could feel that the fucking was a cry of pain, and wondered at it. Was hurt by it. Afterwards, he didn't light a cigarette and blow smoke rings at the ceiling as usual: he just stared at me. "I think you'd better let him go," he said. (I'd told him the whole story before we got our clothes off.)

"I can't."

"You can't go on like this."

"There's no choice."

"There are always choices." Mike frowned. "But . . . having said that . . . I'm in a no-win situation too."

"What do you mean?"

He had, he thought, met the Mr Right he'd been hoping would appear one day in the distant future. He'd not been looking: it had just simply happened. At a dinner party. They arranged to meet next evening; and they talked for hours. Met the next day, and the next, and at the week-end drove to Cambridge. Mike's old university; it was, he said, as if he was showing Danny a period of his life: offering himself. Danny had recently broken up with a lover, a relationship of some four years—the lover was a lecturer at Queen Charlotte; did I know him?

"Is this guy—Danny—deeply into shiatsu?"

"Yes." Mike looked surprised. "Who told you?"

"I'm one of Danny's . . . what do you call them? Patients?"

"Really!" We then said what a small world it was, and other similar clichés; but it occurred to me that the gay world actually was small, even in as large and amorphous a city as London—it wasn't infrequent that new friends knew your old friends, were sometimes their ex-lovers, even their current lovers. "We spent the night in a hotel in Cambridge," Mike said. "It was—you could say —pretty good." I felt, absurdly, a little jealous pang. About both of them.

"So why have you let me get into your bed?" I asked.

"Because I haven't made up my mind, not one hundred per cent. He and I . . . we'd be . . . explosive. An explosion that destroys us? Or the opposite . . . forges something like steel? I'm thinking about it. There's . . . one very obvious complication of course."

"HIV positive."

"Yes. He screwed me. And I didn't tell him."

"Jesus, Michael! Why ever *not*? You've destroyed it before it's begun, haven't you? It . . . it must be possible, these days, to go to bed with someone new and say

. . . look, I don't know anything about your previous partners; you don't know anything about mine . . . it's too great a risk, so why don't we use contraceptives? Any sane, decent, honourable man would think that made sense, surely!"

"We *did* go through all that. And neither of us had a condom."

"So . . . what's wrong with safe sex?"

"That's what we intended. And just got carried away, I suppose. Before I knew where I was, my legs were over his shoulders and I was having the living daylights fucked out of me."

"Jesus, Michael!" I said again. "What are you going to do?"

"I don't know." He sighed, brushed my skin with his fingers, then buried his face in the sweat of my crotch. After a while he looked up, shifted, and lay on my chest. My arms stroked his back. "The damage may have been done . . . he now has the virus, perhaps. If I tell him . . . that's it, for sure—the end of the affair. If I don't tell him . . . we carry on . . . and maybe a relationship. *The* relationship."

"With always churning around inside you the knowledge that you could be the cause of his death. He's twenty-three. The same age as Kim. Why did he . . . let himself?"

"He said, oh, probably it didn't matter."

"I can understand the temptation, Mike. I just hope . . . I never fall for it. Sorry! That's dreadfully holier than thou! I don't mean to be sanctimonious."

"It's alright. I am . . . guilty . . . of a certain moral cowardice."

"It's you and I who should be having the big affair, instead of ruining other people's lives. Why aren't we? We shouldn't be messing about with kids like Danny and Kim."

"Perhaps we will," he said, "one of these days. At the moment . . . we seem to be too involved elsewhere."

"Our bodies couldn't be closer than they are this minute."

He put his hand on my balls, then stroked my cock. "Bodies are not enough. Our hearts and minds are with two other people."

"Can I stay till morning? I don't think I can face Kim right now."

"He's probably sleeping at Katya's. *With* Katya. Yes, stay. Please."

He switched off the light, and I curled round him. Some time later, I said, "Are you comfortable?"

"I always am with you," he answered.

"I guess I love you. In a sort of way."

"It's mutual, David. But don't let's do anything for the wrong reason.

> " 'The last temptation is the greatest treason:
> To do the right deed for the wrong reason.' "

"Eliot. Yes. Ouch and touché."

Kim had elastoplast on various parts of his face and forehead. "All superficial cuts," he said. "Well . . . I guess I deserved it." I apologised, but he said I needn't; he could well understand why I'd behaved like that. "I'm the one who has to apologise," he went on. "I don't know what I'm doing or why I'm doing it . . . I know it hurts you. My existence just seems out of control. Maybe I'll be back on course when I get the test result."

It was a long time coming: mine had taken a week, but a fortnight now went by without a word from the hospital. Next week we were going to Spain. I hoped the result wouldn't arrive till after we left; if it was positive, I feared he'd refuse to come on the trip, or, at the very least, make life such hell it would be a waste of money and effort.

We decided a car was essential, so I booked my Toyota onto the Plymouth-Santander ferry, and paid for two passengers. I was not looking forward to the crossing, as it lasted twenty-four hours; once there, however, we could tour around, perhaps even drive over the whole country, searching for "old" things: castles, cathedrals, ruins of all sorts. I very much wanted to see the Moorish monuments in Andalusia. I worked out a rough itinerary; Kim, not knowing anything about Spain, had no particular preferences, and suggested I should do the planning. But he was eager and excited: a vacation in "Europe" —he had picked up from Katya the idea that Europe was elsewhere—would be just great, he said. Just *great*! He seemed a lot more cheerful.

We weren't due back in England till after the beginning of the autumn term. I'd arranged for Katya to stand in for me, which was fine with the chairman of my depart-

ment: I'd introduced them years ago, and he'd always
been impressed with her ability and knowledge. It was
only for a week, so not much harm would be done to anybody if she found she couldn't cope with my work. I
didn't tell the chairman where I was going, or why; I needed, I said, time off for "personal and private reasons". He
said so long as my classes were covered it was O.K. Or-
ganizing this with Katya was the only communication I'd
had with her since the morning after Kim's birthday, and
it was on the phone, not face to face. "I can't speak to you
. . . yet," I said. "I don't know what you're doing with
him or why. But I'm terribly hurt. I feel betrayed."

"I can understand that," she said. "Though we *must*
talk soon."

"Sure."

For the night of his birthday wasn't the only night
he'd stayed at her flat. In the past two weeks he'd divid-
ed his time more or less evenly between me and her. I pretended to accept this: made little comment to him, though
I asked him once which of us he preferred in bed. "I
couldn't say," he replied. "It's as different as chalk and
cheese. But I enjoy both." He now used contraceptives
with me: was that, I wondered, a bit like bolting the stable
door after the horse has gone? We would have to discuss
the whole thing properly, sooner or later: perhaps in
Spain, or after the test result. My apparent condoning,
however, of what he was up to helped in other areas of our
lives. We were able to chat in an ordinary fashion about
ordinary things—TV programmes, the weather, tourist
London, and so on. But we were drifting apart: when he

wasn't with Katya, he wasn't all the time with me. He went sightseeing on his own, for instance, and some evenings I stayed upstairs preparing work for my autumn classes, while he watched television in the lounge. On one occasion I left him on his own all night: I went round to Mike's and slept there.

Mike was curious about Katya's motives. Though she'd agreed with me that old friends were, any day of the week, better than lovers, she'd gone on to query the any. Perhaps she thought now that the reverse was true, that a chance to be fucked by a virile, sexy young man was a lot more important than old friendship. "Maybe she sees herself as an amateur therapist," Mike said. "She could think she's trying to do you a favor—helping to restore Kim to some kind of equilibrium."

"What about the hurt to me in the process?"

"Well . . . David's shoulders are broad, she may be saying. Experienced older man. Much more so than Kim."

"That's all very well. Should schizos and paranoids have first claim on our sympathies? Just because I haven't behaved like Kim doesn't mean hurting me is of no consequence! Prick me, Mike, and I bleed too!"

"I don't know what she's doing," he said. "You'll have to ask her."

"I will. But not yet."

"I'm tired." He started to take his clothes off. "You can sleep with me if you want . . . but I'm not going to make love."

"Why not?"

"I now have a commitment to Danny. One to one."

We looked at each other rather solemnly. "Have you told him . . . about your test?"

"No." He sighed. "And I shan't. On my head be it."

"Where is he?"

"Out of town. He's gone to see his parents, and he's staying overnight."

Shiatsu. Tomorrow we would be driving to Plymouth, en route for Spain. It was good: serene, restful; I fell asleep in the middle of it. And woke to find my head rocking in Danny's hands: mother. He smiled his loveliest smile, and I repressed a strong urge to pull his face down to mine and kiss him passionately.

As we drank our tea—elderflower on this occasion —he said, "No knots of tension today. But there's something wrong with you. As if you ached dully, all over, inside."

"Perhaps I do," I answered. "How's Mike?"

He laughed. "Changing the subject! He's O.K. . . . he's . . . gorgeous! He says you used to . . . to have sex together."

"I mentioned him once—the man I said I felt bad about because I told him he couldn't sleep with me while Kim was here."

"Oh!" He had not guessed that person was Mike, apparently, but he didn't look worried, or annoyed. "He's a beautiful human being," he said.

"Is he?" I have one big reservation, I said to myself.

"I'm lucky. Very, very lucky."

I could hardly tell him that because of Mike he could be HIV positive. I felt sad, almost wretched: Danny, attractive in every way, experiencing love's young dream, point, purpose, and fulfillment, was ignorant of the worm at the centre. The virus in the apple. I thought of a book I'd once read: Holbrook's *Human Hope and the Death Instinct*. And Keats:

> Now more than ever seems it rich to die,
>> To cease upon the midnight with no pain,
>>> While thou art pouring forth thy soul abroad
>> In such an ecstasy!

The Romantics, I said to myself, may have amused themselves by playing about with ideas that linked love and death: in the gay 1980s, that link was all too real.

"Look after each other," I said. "And take care."

He kissed me goodbye. "We do. We will."

I had never been to Spain. I'd always said I wouldn't go while Franco was in power—I hated the idea of travelling through places ruled by a fascist tyrant—and since democracy had arrived ten years ago I'd somehow not got round to it. Spain turned out to be very much my kind of country: I loved it—the abrupt changes of landscape, the red-tiled roofs that time had forgotten, the weeds and storks' nests on the towers of dilapidated Baroque churches, the mountains in the south snow-capped all

year long, the central plain the colour of apricot, swelter-
ing, dusty, silent. The flowers on patios and in window-
boxes. The heat. The tinkle of goat-bells. It was a trea-
sure-house of crumbling works of art; not even the Spaniards themselves, I thought, could begin to catalogue all
the ruined mansions and castles, all the paintings in mu-
seums and churches. The clashes of culture and history:
in coal-mining, socialist Oviedo, eighth-century Visi-
gothic churches still intact, in use; the contrast between
grave, disapproving Burgos—Franco's stuffy Civil War
capital—and the hedonistic, sensuous street life and
colour of Seville; the difference between Córdova's
mosque, floating like a Bedouin tent in stone, and the
soaring French-style medieval glass at León. More than
any other place, Toledo mirrored it all—Roman relics,
Arab fort and mosque, Jewish synagogue, Christian cathedral. So many Spains, sometimes living in harmony,
but mostly over the centuries wounding each other: the
Civil War the great powder-keg that destroyed them all by
burning them into one, yet curiously leaving few traces of
itself for the tourist to see—only beggars, one-legged
blind men, mourning women. Black and white: the whitewashed houses of town squares dozing in noon heat, their
inhabitants in black berets, black suits, black frocks,
black shawls. We saw Don Quixote's windmills: I could
understand, looking at the immense, breezy plain of
Castile, why he tilted at them—Spain can breed mad-
ness. The absurd slogan of the Civil War: *¡Viva la muerte!*
Long live death! Philip the Second, in crazy El Escorial rul-
ing the whole world on the principles of accountancy.

And only Spain could have a queen called Isabella the Nymphomaniac. Spain itself is a castle in Spain, mad as a dream.

Kim loved it too. The houses in Cuenca built on top of, indeed hanging over, a gorge hundreds of feet deep; Santiana del Mar so impossibly picturesque he said it couldn't be real, that it must be a film set; the cardinals' hats on tombs in Toledo cathedral like bloodied mouths or Flanders poppies; the gardens of El Generalife, yes, bright with sinuous rills and incense-bearing trees and not at all like the burned gardens of Los Gatos, but he remembered, as we sat under a palm tree drinking orange juice, our conversation that summer night, and said—it was the first time since HIV that there was any genuine feeling in the words—"I love you, David. I *love* you!" But in Madrid, when I suggested we might go to a disco, he refused. He loved dancing and so did I; once at the Hippodrome in London we had footslogged for two hours—he had seemed drunk with the music: delirious, and abandoned with *me*. There's almost no pleasure, I remember thinking, like dancing with my lover. Now—it was like the petty spitefulness with the box of chocolates—discos were not allowed. "I wouldn't enjoy it," he said. "The memories would hurt."

I did most of the driving: he'd never driven a car with the steering wheel on the right-hand side, nor one with a stick-shift gear, and was nervous about it. After the caprices of bad Spanish roads, and the nightmare of finding a way through the narrow twisting streets of medieval inner cities, I was sometimes by early evening fit for nothing but flopping into the nearest bar for a few glasses of valdepeñas or rioja. He took it upon himself, therefore, to search out reasonably priced hotels and good restaurants. Neither of us spoke any Spanish, so, armed with a phrasebook, he would set off in Segovia, Salamanca, Zamora, Jaén, Cácares, to execute this task, and took an almost childish pleasure in hitting upon something we'd both like. "I've done it again!" he'd say. "I've done it again! Haven't I?" He was particularly proud of the room with our own private balcony in Toledo, and the Hotel Manuel de Falla just by Falla's house in Granada, which had a spectacular view of the city and the snow-covered peaks of the nearby mountains. He'd never heard of Falla until I'd said, a few days before, how much I loved the music of Spain's most famous composer, and he seemed delighted that I was pleased we were staying next door to the great man's house. While he was away on this errand I sat at a table outside a bar, drinking grenadine and watching the world go by. I exchanged prolonged glances with an attractive street urchin. Kim returned while this performance was going on, and said, "Is that your cruising look?"

"I suppose so," I answered.

"I've never seen it before." He glared at me. "It makes me very jealous!"

You sleep some of the time with Katya, I said to myself, and some of the time with me; yet you're jealous if I just glance, for a few seconds longer than usual, at a sexy boy in a Granada street. One morality for you, a different one for me. That's not love. But that night, in the Manuel de Falla, we made superb love: hours that chased away each other's fears, soothed worries, alleviated stress. Most nights, however, we didn't. Our senses were filled with good meals, rioja, what we'd seen and done: we were too tired.

The most beautiful place we visited was Zahara de los Membrillos—Zahara of the Quince Trees. We saw this Andalusian village while we were driving to Ronda, its houses tumbling down a mountainside like a white waterfall: on the summit was a ruined castle, which was, our guidebook told us, a tenth-century Arab fort. We hadn't planned to stop, but it was too magnificent to miss.

"I want to stay the night here," Kim said.

He went off, as usual, to find a place. This turned out to be the Pensión Gonzago, the only inn in the village. There was no restaurant, but the patrona of the Gonzago, Señora Rodriguez, would cook us dinner. We climbed up to the Arab fort, past cactuses and late-flowering poppies, and absorbed the view: the pinnacle of Spain it seemed to be up there, mountains, folds and folds of them, falling away from us on every side. Grey earth, dark olive groves. Zahara, underneath us, was now more terracotta than white—we were looking down on the spider's web patterns of its roof slates. We made love against the battlements, and afterwards I stared up at the sky: evening sky, cool, colour draining from it, though flushed towards the west. It would be a chill night. There was one lone star. I was at peace: absolutely content.

"Tell me what you're thinking," I said. "A peseta for them." They couldn't, I imagined, be anything other than happy, satisfied thoughts. Loving thoughts.

"I was dialoguing in my head," he answered.

"With whom?"

"Katya."

I was surprised. I hadn't thought about Katya for days. "Was it a nice conversation?"

"I miss her."

"Were you missing her when we made love just now?"

He stared down at the church tower, which was littered with the usual storks' nests and buddleia bushes, then up at the sky. "Yes," he said.

I'm a masochist, I told myself. Stop asking questions! "Do you always think of her when you're screwing me?"

"Not always."

"Do you love her?"

"Yes. Oh . . . yes."

So, I said to myself, that is the score. Did he know what love meant, experience it as I did, and had done in the past? I doubted it very much. He had no compassion, no responsibility, no empathy, no commitment, for me or for her: merely lust and selfishness. We satisfied his body, provided a home to live in, were a free meal ticket and an introduction to the ancient sites of Europe. He had, it is true, a respect for our intelligence and our experience of life, and in Katya's case, a more general respect that HIV had dimmed in his view of me. He will return to Katya in the end, I said to myself. She isn't the beast who might infect him; he feels safer with her because of that. He thinks if he stays too long with me he'll be positive too; she doesn't have that virus, is not a death threat.

There is no point, David, in dreaming about growing old with this man. He doesn't love you. Doesn't love anyone. Only himself. Himself first, himself last. He's only here for the ride.

Mike is just the same. He loves Danny, he says, but he knows he could be infecting him with a killer disease. That's not love. It's a desire for security, pleasure, and the status of being one half of a couple. He doesn't love Danny. Doesn't love anyone. Only himself. Himself first, himself last.

Love is something a lot more giving, and caring.

I made my way slowly down to Zahara and its quince trees, leaving Kim to stare at the sky.

« SEVEN »

B ut I loved him, was bound, committed to him. That
was all renewed as we talked over Señora Rodriguez's dinner (the best meal, and the cheapest, of the
whole trip), and as he attempted, afterwards, to commu-
nicate with her and her many friends—all middle-aged
women dressed in black from houses up and down the
street, who had popped in, maybe, to observe this unusual curiosity in Zahara of the Quince Trees, an americano
and an inglés. Helped only by his Spanish phrase-book,
he elicited the information that these people had known
one another all their lives, were mostly related—second
cousin, third cousin—and that they liked to spend their
evenings together while their men-folk drank at the bar in
the plaza mayor. Kim's delight in working all this out was
infectious: he is sweet; I do love him, I said to myself.

The conversation turned to politics. Not surprising-
ly, perhaps, in this most politically passionate and
sophisticated of nations, but it puzzled Kim. "Felipito

sí!" the women said many times, smiling, nodding,
thumbs up; "Juan Carlos—no!" (mouths turned down,
heads quite still, thumbs inverted). From which I gathered
they disapproved of the monarchy and were all good
socialists, Felipito being the nickname of Felipe
Gonzalez, Spain's prime minister. Their British equiv-
alents, a group of boarding-house proprietresses, would,
I said to myself, be as much of the right as these women
were of the left. But this was Zahara de los Membrillos,
Andalusia, not Blackpool, Lancs: traditionally
socialist—indeed anarchist—territory during the days of
the Republic and Civil War. I was surprised, however,
that they did not think well of Juan Carlos: but maybe Republican sentiments and memories die very hard. Kim, of
course, was unaware of these nuances. He was bewildered now, for the women, having asked him what he
thought of Ronald Reagan, were expressing their own
views on the actor in the White House—that he was quite
dreadful, the greatest threat to world peace since the Lord
knew when. Kim had no opinions, one way or the other,
on the subject of the American President, and was
amazed that these women should be at all interested in
him.

He managed to turn the conversation to an easier
topic, the places we had visited, and was answering questions like what did we do in Madrid; and had we seen the
Alhambra, what did we think of Córdova's mosque? I
contributed almost nothing: just sat and enjoyed watching the child-like pleasure on all the faces, the women's
as much as Kim's.

"Do you like it here?" I asked, when we were in bed.

"It's enchanted. Holy."

I looked at the simple pattern of the floor-tiles, the Mozarabic design on the water jug, and listened to the silence of the night outside. I thought of cactuses, the tenth-century tower, the sunset, the rioja we had drunk, the distant olive groves, Felipito sí, the marigolds and geraniums blooming on the dusty patios. Spain. Yes, a holy place. Though in my memory it would always be entwined with Kim, it wouldn't be an inextricable entanglement. Spain was so rich, so varied, so congenial, I could return here, I said to myself, either with him or with another man, or alone, maybe to this very house and ask how Felipito was doing, sleep in this same room: and be happy.

But the next morning we began a conversation that went on for several days, in Ronda and Seville, and as we drove up the valley of the Guadalquivir, back through Córdova to Ciudad Real and Toledo; "Don't leave me" was its theme.

"I love you, but not enough to live with you," he said for the nth time, as he photographed me by an escallonia hedge in the little garden outside Toledo's mosque.

"If I lose you, I have nothing."

"Oh, you'll find somebody else quite easily."

"Thanks. How patronising."

"You're gorgeous, David. Sensational! You have the most beautiful legs I've ever seen." (They were all right, I said to myself on a good day, and now, suntanned and visible—I was wearing shorts—they probably didn't look too bad. For someone of my age.) "That iron grey hair! It's a miracle there isn't a procession of young men wanting to rip your clothes off."

"It has nothing to do with legs and hair," I said. "Aren't you forgetting I'm HIV positive? Suppose I did find somebody else, and he's not just cute, but compatible and interesting, and if all those other ifs worked out like could I love him, and he me: how do I say I've produced the antibodies? And *when* do I say it?" Danny came into my head at this moment. "He'd run a mile. If he had any sense."

"You could find another man who's positive."

"Oh. Advertise for him?"

"People do. I've seen adverts in the gay papers. 'HIV positive, forty, London, grey-haired, blue-eyed, attractive, seeks similar for long-lasting relationship.' Or you could contact the Terrence Higgins Trust."

" 'Dear Terrence Higgins, I have a problem. I'm looking for a Kim look-alike who's antibody positive . . . ' Don't be such an arsehole! I want you and *only* you."

But if he did leave me, I could, I suppose, reply to such advertisements. Or put one in the papers myself. I could meet others in situations like mine, perhaps, through Terrence Higgins and Body Positive. After I'd got over the break-up, flushed Kim out of my system. Which could take months. Years.

"I put all my eggs in one basket," he said again. "You smashed them. I wanted you and only you . . . once upon a time."

"A time of innocence. A garden of innocence. Like this dear little place." Warm, rich scents. I looked at the flowers, the year's late bees.

"I feel . . . betrayed."

"Betrayed! Why? I've don't nothing . . . absolutely nothing . . . to hurt you! To hurt *us!*"

"But you have."

"I didn't know! How could I have known? It wasn't deliberate."

"It makes no difference."

I shook my head in disbelief. "I don't understand you. Or if I try to understand . . . my reasoning moves along lines that are not . . . very flattering. That Katya's a better *offer.* Security . . . a home in America to return to. And no risk . . . she won't give you AIDS. You're weighing us up like a business proposition: which is the better bargain? It's not *love!*"

"Perhaps love isn't enough. Not any longer. Not now."

"What's that supposed to mean? You're condemning me . . . to a very lonely life. It isn't *fair!* Does it make you happy?"

"Nothing's fair. And it doesn't make me happy . . . to think of you . . . in the afterwards of us. It makes me feel guilty . . . I'd like you to believe that." He squeezed my hand, then kissed me. "I don't know what I shall do, to be quite honest. I don't yet know if I'll leave you . . . if I'll live with Katya."

"You only want her because you think she's safe!"

"I do love you, David."

"No, you don't. You're simply out for what you can get. Right now . . . a free trip to Spain."

He sighed. "Can we take a little walk? I want to see the synagogue."

It was one of the most interesting discoveries of the whole trip. The usual key-hole arches of Mozarabic buildings, but with an almost effortless symmetry and grace—Christian, Moor, and Jew blended in perfect harmony. It belonged to another Eden, centuries dead, when Toledo was an outpost of the Emirate of Córdova, ruled by benign sultans who practised a religious toleration unknown in the rest of the world; a product of the time before the Reconquest of Isabella and Ferdinand, those Catholic monarchs who gave Spain its present frontiers, and who invented the Inquisition. Toledo's Jews were expelled from their Eden. I decided I much preferred the woman of no importance, Isabella the Nymphomaniac, to the woman of fixed ideas, Isabella the Catholic.

"Another holy place," Kim said, touching its walls.

"Don't leave me, Kim. It isn't that if you do I have nothing. That's not a good line of argument, true though it surely is. I just . . . want you. You, you, you."

He held me in his arms. "You see . . . I am with you still."

"For always?"

"There is no always." He kissed me. "You're a good man. Generous, loving, thoughtful, concerned, interesting . . . but . . ."

"But?"

"But."

There were moments, however, when I felt I had got him back completely. In Plasencia, the cathedral was closed for major repairs to its crumbling structure, so we sat on a bench outside it, and watched the storks on its towers. Grotesquely standing on one leg, or taking off in ungainly fashion, their legs trailing behind them: they looked, in flight, like giant crane flies. They stabbed each other with their bills, in annoyance maybe, or affection, or it could have simply been functional—removing parasites that itched. The marvel was when they clattered their beaks. A rapid tap-tap-tap-tap-tap sound, not exactly metallic, more like a woodpecker boring into a tree branch. An urgent, significant sound that seemed to convey all kinds of emotions incomprehensible to us.

"Amazing!" Kim said, all child-like wonder again. "I shan't forget this as long as I live!"

"Stork talk."

"Moments with you . . . so many I'll preserve for ever."

"For ever?"

"You and me for ever you're asking? Oh yes, yes . . . I do want that. I *do* want it!"

Similarly when we were driving away from a not particularly interesting town in a not particularly interesting part of red Castile: we turned a corner, and there, dumped by the side of the road, was an ancient aeroplane, a large sign on one of its wings—CAFÉ. We stopped for a beer, and talked to the proprietor who had once worked for an insurance firm in Liverpool. He spoke English (the only Spaniard we met who did) with a strong

Scouse accent; business wasn't too good, he said, despite the unusual appeal to passers-by of a drink in an
aeroplane cockpit. He was thinking of moving to
somewhere on the coast, Valencia perhaps, but he
hadn't yet worked out how to do it—the plane didn't fly:
he'd got rid of the engines to make room for his drink
store.

"You're right," Kim said, when we drove away.
"This country is *mad!*"

"Another for ever?"

"Yes." He smiled. "As with you and me. For ever."

I've won the battle, I said to myself. Or at least it's
going my way. But in Santiana del Mar, on the evening
before we sailed for Plymouth, he said, when he saw me
looking at Pablo, the teenage son of the house in which we
were spending the night—a slim, tall youth with curly,
shoulder-length hair and sexy black eyes—"As I told
you, David: you'll have *no* problems."

"Stay with me."

He didn't answer.

He was positive. That was the news (like me, he was told
over the phone) that greeted us in London. In my bedroom
hung a poster I'd bought in Amsterdam—it was an adver-
tisement for a disco, and its caption read: *Hey! Are you
gay? See you Monday!*, and in small letters beneath this
were the words *At the Flora Palace.* The picture was a
photograph of two men stripped to the waist; one stood
behind the other, arms round the man in the foreground,

hands either resting on top of his lover's jeans, or perhaps starting to undo the zip. It wasn't pornographic, not even erotic. I liked it as an uninhibited celebration of male gayness. Kim, for some reason I could never work out, thought it offensive. The first thing he did when he heard the bad news was to tear the poster into little bits. Times change: in its place now hangs a picture of two more attractive men, nude—it's altogether more erotic—and, I think, about to make love. I say I think, as the photograph doesn't include their legs and the lower parts of their torsos. It comes from the Terrence Higgins Trust, and its caption is: *Safer Sex.*

Kim locked himself in the bathroom, and cried for nearly an hour. I banged on the door and pleaded with him to open it, but I was wasting my time; he wouldn't answer, let alone permit me to come in. He emerged eventually, and went downstairs. I heard him speak to someone on the phone, Katya presumably. I was in the lounge, trying to read a book, but I could hardly see the print. "I'm going out," he said, "and I'm not sure when I'll be back."

I spent the afternoon teaching my first classes of the term, which forced me to concentrate on matters other than Kim. But conversations with some of my colleagues left me sour. Katya had done a marvellous week's work, they said; the students adored her and nobody had missed me at all. And, from those in the know—the American kid was clearly doing wonders for me; I had never looked so good. So relaxed!

Six o'clock; I had just arrived home when Kim

called. He was at Katya's, was eating there and staying
the night. He'd be back tomorrow, to sort out some of his
things—he was leaving in the afternoon for two weeks in
Brittany—with her.

I said: "Oh."

Time I did some sorting out as well, I said to myself
as I cooked dinner. Katya, to start with. But how? What
would I say, and where and when? Having eaten, and
drunk a whole bottle of wine, and thought about the great
moments of the past she and I had shared—the pleasures,
the confidences, the fun, the jokes, the nights out, the
nights in—I found I'd worked myself up into a tremendous rage. I just wanted to smash both her and Kim into
the middle of next week. Not that I would. But it was time
for a showdown, and when was better than now?

I drove to Alameda Street, descended the area
steps, and knocked on the door. The curtains were shut,
but not pulled tightly together; I could see a table laid for
two, with lit candles. No sign of the occupants—in the
kitchen, I assumed, cooking. I knocked again. After a
while the curtains were pulled open, and there was Kim.
In the background Katya stood. "Who is it?" she asked.

"David."

She left the room. "Let me in," I said.

"No," he answered. "It isn't the right time."

"I need to talk to Katya."

"Not now. Go away, David." We stared at each
other. He seemed to be amused, was smiling: a nasty little glint of vindictive triumph in his eyes. He is not a good
person, I said to myself. In fact a real copper-bottomed

shit. And what about her? What morass had all those years of friendship hidden? "Are you going to make a scene?" he said. "You've been drinking, I suppose."

I didn't reply. The wind sobbed in the area, lifted a few dead leaves and bits of paper, whirled them, let them fall. I shivered. An extraordinary moment, a for ever for me—the black beast outside in the cold October darkness, not to be allowed in at any cost; the wicked intruder who'd disturb the warmth, the candle-light, the tête-à-tête between lovers. Kim's smile widened. He is really enjoying this, I thought. What a *bastard* he is! I could have strangled him then and there; been delighted to do so: the urge was that strong.

One kiss, however, and the beast would turn into a beautiful prince.

That didn't happen. Of course. "Go away!" he said, again.

"I'll kill you!" I said. "And when I've done that, I'll kill her!"

His smile vanished, and he swept the curtains shut. As I walked up to the pavement, I heard him lock and bolt the inside of the door.

I hoped, as I drove to Muswell Hill, that Danny would not be there; I needed to unburden myself to Mike, and at least be held and kissed, even if he wouldn't let me have sex. If Danny was present, I couldn't, of course, say anything that referred to HIV, and that meant, in effect, I couldn't say anything at all. Nor be held and kissed.

Danny was there, sitting on the other side of the table where I'd often sat, the remains of dinner in front of
him. Wine glasses, and candle-light too: everyone seems
to have a thing about candles this evening, I said to myself. The usual mischievous eyes—he looked proprieto-
rial, as if he owned the place.

"He's moved in with me," Mike explained. "Though
I don't think we'll stay here long; it isn't really big
enough for two."

"A bit further to come for shiatsu," Danny said.

"We're going to look for somewhere
else . . . maybe buy a flat. Do you want some wine?"

"I'd better not," I answered. "I've already drunk a
whole bottle. Oh . . . why the fuck shouldn't I? Yes,
I'll have a glass."

Danny went out to the kitchen. Mike stared at me,
and said, "What's the matter?" During the few moments
we were alone, I was able to say that Kim was positive too,
that he and Katya were going to Brittany, that neither of
them would let me in when I called just now at Alameda
Street.

"God! What a mess!" Mike muttered. "But not another word, please . . . not a word . . . Danny knows
nothing."

Danny returned with the wine. "Did you have a good
trip?" he asked.

"Oh yes, very good. Very good indeed."

"You look superb. That suntan!" He smiled at me
again, holding the glance just a little longer than was
necessary. As if he was saying: you could have had me if

you'd wanted me—but it's too late.

I stayed there an hour. The talk was all of themselves, their plans, and what they'd achieved already.
The revealing of little intimacies to one who was, I guess,
an old friend; the comments very-much-in-love lovers
can't resist making to those they think they know
well—to celebrate this beautiful structure they were
building. For example: Danny wouldn't stop squeezing
the toothpaste tube at the wrong end; the way to make
Mike happy was always to have dinner on time; Mike had
learned to rinse the dishes after washing them; Danny
had discovered the pleasures of house plants, Mike the
pleasure of sex in the morning. I watched and listened,
envious and horrified: how could Mike enjoy making love
with this man when he knew that each occasion could
pass on the virus? How could he talk about saving money
for the deposit on a flat when in a year or two he—or both
of them—could be dead? What would I feel in Mike's
position? I felt tainted and contaminated enough as it
was: sure I could, if I wanted to, have a safe-sex one-night
stand without mentioning HIV and feel O.K. about it, but
getting *involved* with somebody who wasn't in the same
situation as myself: unthinkable! Impossible!

It occured to me that I really didn't know Mike all
that well. Despite the mental compatibility and the
similar interests, our meeting-ground had first and fore-
most been in bed. As a moral being, I'd assumed he was
the same as myself: the usual mistake. What was it I'd
once said to him? He and I should be having the big affair
instead of running around with kids like Kim and Danny.

What nonsense! I could no more have an affair, now, with Mike than fly to the moon. I felt too much contempt.

Safe-sex one-night stand without mentioning HIV. Why not? If I didn't, there'd be nobody in my bed for two weeks, and quite probably after that. For ever? Hmmm.

On the way home I went into Traffic; just to see what was there, I said to myself—I hadn't been in for months. Very busy, as it often was, not so clonish as the L.A., or boring like some of the pubs outside Central London. Always a good young crowd, and always cruisy. What was I looking for? An attractive man—it goes without saying—but one I wouldn't want to see again, nor he me: a nice body and no brains, he wanting someone simply because he didn't care to go home alone. A man to cuddle up to in bed, and do nothing with—the lateness of the hour, I could tell him, or I'd had too much to drink (which was certainly true)—or perhaps we could enjoy a pleasurable wank together. No more than that.

My wishes were not granted. The gods are undoubtedly not at the moment favouring me, I said to myself. It was Simon I took home, a good-looking twenty-seven-year-old teacher of maladjusted children, an extremely interesting, intelligent and charming guy, who was not, he said, at all into one-night stands. He wanted a lover. I listened to his biography—curious how on these occasions many of us tell the person we've picked up the details of our past love lives, whereas there are people we've known for years to whom we never mention a word about this area of ourselves—and thought: this is exactly the kind of man, before Kim, before HIV, I would have wanted to see again. I watched him as he took off his clothes: a beautiful body. He stroked my face, kissed me very gently. The effect was extraordinary. With most men who kiss you the experience is pleasing—all the familiar, usual sensations; then along comes one whose touch is quite fantastic: I can only think of clichés like blowing one's mind. Simon was one of these rare few. I suddenly felt awake, quickened in every pore of my skin. Erect immediately. I just wanted to surrender—fuck or be fucked; it didn't matter.

"Christ," he whispered. It was the same for him. "What do you want?"

"You mean, right now?"

"No. If this is just a one-off . . . then . . . I'd rather we didn't. You've told me so little about yourself, except for your work, your holiday in Spain. Do you have a lover? You haven't even said that. Did you go to Spain with him? I can't stand pointless screwing . . . It makes me feel degraded."

"I'm sorry. I've got problems . . . *serious* problems."

"Do you want to tell me?"

"Yes. But I can't, not just at the moment. I *will* tell you . . . some other time."

"There'll be another time?"

"Yes." I stroked his cock. "Shall we do this for now?"

"O.K."

Even that was quite sensational.

Not only—prior to HIV—a man I'd want to see

again, but a man I could fall for, begin a relationship with. My thoughts, as I drifted into sleep, were: I'm a sexual outcast. That's my for ever. A sexual outcast. The S.T.D. adviser came into my mind. "We tell all gay men they should take the test." I wanted to beat him to a pulp. What a sodding, fucking, shitty catastrophe! A sodding, fucking, shitty life to come! Till the disease killed me. Two years? Ten years? Could be a sodding, fucking, shitty life till I died of old age thirty or forty years on. My one chance of happiness: to find another like me. Through Body Positive—the only meeting-ground. Our chances, normally, weren't prodigious, ninety per cent of men being straight, and what percentage of the gay ten per cent was positive, and without a lover, and who wanted a lover? And who might fancy me, and I him? Almost no per cent.

And here was this beautiful man in my bed, asleep, trusting me enough to let himself stay till morning with my arms wrapped round him. Yes, Mike . . . I certainly know the temptation. But I will not. I will *not*!

After breakfast we exchanged telephone numbers, and said we would ring. A common scenario, but this time it was sincere. He went off to work, and I listened to the silence. I'd have felt elated, once. Not now.

Kim arrived, to pack his bags for Brittany. He did not take all his possessions, merely what he needed for the trip. So he wasn't planning to move in with Katya, just yet.

I didn't ask for details, such as how they were travelling, where they would stay, or whether they were hiring a car when they got to wherever it was they were going—Rennes? Morlaix? Roscoff? I didn't even bother to find out when they expected to return.

"Katya wanted to know if you have an answer to this question," he said. "A character in one of Chekhov's plays—I don't remember which play or which character, and I couldn't pronounce it even if I did—says Balzac was born in Berdichev, Russia, when really he was born in Tours, France. Do you know why Chekhov thought it was Berdichev?"

"You can tell her," I said, "to stuff Chekhov up her arse."

She was misquoting, in fact. Chebutykin in *Three Sisters* says Balzac's *marriage* took place in Berdichev. Her mind, it would appear, was not at the moment wholly on her work.

« EIGHT »

I wouldn't say the two weeks of their absence in Brittany dragged by at a snail's pace, but, nevertheless, Kim and Katya were always in my thoughts—at college, and when I was alone in the house, or at shiatsu with Danny, or out with Simon. First thing in the morning, in fact, and last thing at night. What was going on there preoccupied me—not whether they were enjoying Dinard or Mont St Michel, or even the fucking (though it hurt to think about that, hurt very much; and I tried to push such images out of my head)—but what kind of relationship was being forged, and why: what plans were being made, and did such plans exclude me. It was no good telling myself that Katya-and-Kim was absurd, a non-starter— middle-aged woman, not even young middle-aged, intellectual, cultured, a scholarly university professor shacking up with an inexperienced, illiterate jock of twenty-three who wasn't even very skilled at the only work he'd ever tried. In theory it didn't make sense, but history, literature, and more than one example I knew of, or had heard of, showed that such liaisons could succeed, could even last a lifetime. And . . . it wasn't so different from David-and-Kim, only the gender and ten years. I was fairly sure that, on his return, he would move in with her, which would lead to a colossal row between Katya and me, and maybe a severance of all ties with both of them. I was going to have a colossal row with Katya anyway. Betrayal by a lover was bad enough, but when that involved, was compounded by, maybe caused by one's best friend, it was beyond human endurance to let it pass with no comment.

Simon and I drove up to Cambridge. My suggestion; the first interesting place outside London I could think of —but perhaps I was subconsciously recalling that Mike had told me it was where he and Danny had first made love. Was I needing to make some curious kind of amends for that by taking Simon there *not* to do the same thing? We walked through the college gardens, Queens', King's, Clare, Trinity, St John's—and I told him about HIV positive. Almost trembling as I did so, for I feared his reaction, whatever it would be—contempt, horror, pity: it was sure to be something I didn't want. And I also told him about Mike, and Mike and Danny. And the whole story of my relationship with Kim. It took a long time. We had passed over the Mathematical Bridge, wandered through the courts of Queens' and King's, gazed at the stained glass windows, the fan vaulting and the superb Rubens in King's College chapel, crossed the river and strolled in the gardens of Clare (the best in Cambridge, now a riot of autumn colours), walked under Housman's cherry trees at Trinity, and reached the Wedding Cake of St John's before I finished.

On the Bridge of Sighs, staring down at the Cam, he said, "Tell me again exactly what it means to be antibody positive. I'm sorry . . . I'm ignorant."

"I've been exposed to the virus. I've slept with somebody who was capable of passing the virus on—Mike. And because Kim is positive too, *I'm* capable of passing the virus on. It does *not* mean any of us has AIDS."

"But you could develop it."

"Yes."

"Christ!" He shook his head. "And I thought . . . I'm sorry to put it like this . . . I'd met the man I wanted a relationship with. A commitment. Perhaps I still do . . . want the relationship, I mean; the commitment. Perhaps I still . . . can. I've got to think about it. Got to think!" He banged his fist on the wall. "Tell me . . . is there anything we did in bed the other night that could possibly have infected me?"

"Absolutely nothing."

"Thank God for that!"

"You didn't come in me, nor I in you. No 'exchange of body fluids', as they say. I wouldn't have dreamed of allowing it."

"But we kissed," he said.

"Not a great danger."

And a hundred other questions, as we walked through the courts of St John's and up Trinity Street, over tea in the Copper Kettle, as we looked at the paintings in the

Fitzwilliam, on the drive back to London, in my house that evening. I gave him all the literature I'd acquired from Body Positive, and, more recently, from the Terrence Higgins Trust. He read this while I cooked dinner. Later, he said, picking up one of the leaflets, "It says here: 'Kissing must be very low risk, as nearly all cases of HIV infection have had actual intercourse or received blood and one would expect many unexplained cases if kissing alone could transmit the virus.'"

"Yes," I answered. "What of it?"

"It goes on: 'Live virus has been isolated from saliva and therefore considerable saliva exchange could in theory transmit the virus.'"

"In theory. Does that . . . bother you?"

"Not sure. We have . . . kissed. Rather . . . mmm . . . totally."

"It also says 'must be very low risk'."

"Yes." He stared into the candle flames. (I'd decided not to be left out of this evidently popular activity.)

"Will you . . . stay with me tonight?"

The question was followed by one of the longest silences I think I've ever experienced in an important, intimate conversation. I watched him. A young face, younger-looking than his twenty-seven years; big, solemn blue eyes and blond hair (again!), though not so strikingly blond as either Kim or Mike. A small man physically, small-boned, neat, compact. In appearance waif-like, vulnerable, though not so as a person: he seemed adult, mature; defined. I began to clear up the dirty plates. "Help yourself to a drink," I said. "There's some brandy."

He did so, and said, "I'll stay with you."

The emotion that flooded me was so intense the plates started to rattle against each other. I put them down on the table: I wanted to cry. "What's wrong?" he asked.

"Gratitude. Relief, I suppose."

In the bedroom we undressed, and looked at each other. He smiled, a brief, almost radiant flash, and, running his forefinger down my body, said, "Come on!"

What I wanted was the wild wrestling I had had with Mike on the evening I'd thrown the glass bowl at Kim. For different reasons of course—not to rid myself of pain and distress, be reassured I was not mortal—but to let go completely, to surrender: to be positive (hah!) that I wasn't, at least in the eyes of one good and beautiful human being, an outcast. It didn't happen. He was making love with a person who could cause him to die: it had to be careful, calculated. He let me suck his cock almost to the point of coming, and it was good to know, hearing the sounds of his pleasure, that I was the instrument of those sensations. But he couldn't bring himself to suck me. Orgasm, for both of us, was very safe. And less than satisfying.

"I don't know if I could let you fuck me," he said, "even with a condom. I've got to think about it. David . . . if I don't contact you for a few days . . . even a week or more . . . it isn't that I've decided not to see you again. I have to work this one out, on my own probably . . . though I may talk to some other people. Do you . . . do you understand?"

"Yes."

"You must have gone through hell. You sweet, sad, lovely guy."

I was calmer: more my usual self. Simon had done that. I saw him only once during the rest of the time Kim and Katya were away, though we frequently spoke on the phone. He was still thinking hard, he said, and it wasn't just simply about fucking with condoms; it was—can we have a relationship? He said: "I've been seeing two old friends quite a lot in the past few days, Alan and Nick. Alan has multiple sclerosis and it's made him blind. Nick knew about the M.S. right from the start—Alan could see then. He knows he'll die soon; they both know it. They are . . . quite a couple."

"The parallel is inexact," I said. "Nick didn't infect him."

"It's exact enough to make me think very clearly."

"You are . . . a marvel, Simon. A revelation!"

"Oh yes," he mocked. "A prophet in the wilderness!"

Elihu, the youth of great beauty, who helped Job in his affliction. Though I couldn't quite cast myself in the role of Job, even if I could well imagine Kim and Katya as a pair of Job's comforters.

I was able to immerse myself in my work as a result of all this—grading student assignments, preparing texts, attending a couple of polite, good-behaviour sherry parties for visiting professors, and even doing various bits of dull administration that, in a state of disequilibrium, I would have neglected altogether. In my spare time, I sought out friends I had not seen for a while—Chris, Tony, Keith, Dizzy, and Maria. I didn't mention HIV; I felt I didn't need to at the moment, and perhaps enough people knew anyway—Mike, Kim, Katya, Simon. It was Simon, of course, who had made it unnecessary to talk. And I said nothing to my friends about him. They all expressed surprise, in one way or another, that Kim had disappeared for a fortnight. Their reactions were characteristic: Chris said he knew it wouldn't last, particularly now Kim had been let loose among the Frogs; I must be crazy to have allowed it. Tony said he was sure I needed the rest—I must be knackered, sucked dry, an old man of forty having to service that young, sexy hunk. Keith asked, rather plaintively, if it meant he'd have to prune his roses himself, but Dizzy and Maria were sure it must still be superior Barbara Cartland.

"Barbara Cartland with balls," I said.

"He's lovely," Maria replied. "Angelic."

"If you don't have separations," Dizzy said, "you don't have meetings. When he gets home I'm pretty sure it'll be a terrific night!" They both chuckled.

The night he returned I didn't see him at all, in fact: he stayed at Alameda Street. He rang from there to tell me. "When are you coming *here?*" I asked. "*Are* you coming here?"

"Yes."

"Put Katya on the line, would you?"

A long pause, then Katya's usual gruff "Hi."

"I've got to talk to you," I said.

"O.K. When?"

"Tomorrow. At your flat?"

"Sure. Do you . . . want to be alone? Shall I send him out?"

"Please."

A long, long, conversation, nothing like the great row I'd been expecting, planning in my head. Despite everything, I found I couldn't do that, not with Katya, old friend, old partner in crime as it were, almost sister; and I was relieved we could be so urbane. But it was wary and circuitous to start with, accompanied by much nervous smoking of cigarettes, she breaking off to refill coffee cups, and at one point to check her bank statement—"I don't always get the hang of the British system," she said. "So I need to look at these figures very thoroughly."

I was rather insensitive to what Kim was going through, was her theme. He was neurotically obsessed by AIDS; he had talked of almost nothing else during the entire two weeks in Brittany. "How much are you going to let this dominate you?" she had asked. "Is that all life is now, fear of something that probably won't happen?" He was badly in need of help, in her view, and she didn't know what to do about it. Psychiatry was very expensive, here as much as anywhere, and it was unlikely that the British health service would allow a visiting American to undergo analysis free. *She* couldn't afford it; he had nothing, and neither of them was going to ask me to pay for it. Just as well, I said to myself, because I couldn't and wouldn't. I told her there were support groups that would assist him, people from Terrence Higgins and Body Positive; she knew that, she said, and so did he, but he was not inclined to get in touch with them. Irrational, of course—he said he couldn't face meeting men in the same situation as himself; it would simply reinforce his fears, remind him too much of what was wrong.

"Which perhaps confirms," I said, "something I'd already guessed. He's come to you because you're disease-free. It's an escape from responsibility. I'm still the black beast who gave him the virus—or, at any rate, produced antibodies in his bloodstream—and he can't look at me in any other light. He ignores my many kindnesses. He thinks I'll somehow pollute him further."

She nodded. "Not impossible if he's in contact with your blood or your semen. There's this theory that sex between positive people is dangerous because you can give one another more of your own virus—"

"A theory that's been discounted."

"—or the antigenic drift idea. In every individual the virus can mutate, so you'd pass on a new strain of it."

"Not if you use condoms," I said.

"Sure. He *knows* that . . . but he's so freaked out he still thinks there's a terrible hazard."

"But . . . it's completely selfish . . . he'll have sex with *you*! Because *you're* untainted, it's O.K. for *him*! Doesn't he realise he's as contaminated as I am?"

"Apparently not."

"I'll give him a death sentence?"

"I s'pose."

I tried to control my annoyance. "It's so inconsistent," I said. "He *does* still fuck me. With a condom, sure. He's an egotistical monster."

"No. A very muddled little bag of fears."

"A muddled, little, fearful, egotistical monster."

She didn't answer that, just stared out of the window. "I understand your hurt," she said, after a while. "I understand it very well. But you can shoulder it. He can't."

"What are you getting out of this, Katya? And don't give me the convenient angel of redemption bit. The white goddess stuff."

"I?" She stood, paced up and down, and lit another cigarette. "I don't know what to tell you. Maybe . . . you should ask me some questions, and I'll try to give you some idea."

"Does he love you? Is he *in* love with you?"

"I think so. He says so."

It was very odd, imagining that. Terribly distressing. I could hear him in my head—it was only a few weeks ago—as he came in me: "I love you, David! Jesus Christ, I love you, I *love* you!!" Similarly . . . last night . . . with her? "Do you love him?" I asked.

She sat down, and sighed. "I . . . I need a lot of notice for that one. Can you give me a raincheck?"

"No!"

"O.K." she said. "I fancy him, I enjoy him . . . physically . . . and in all kinds of ways. He's another son. I don't get bored, which, as you know, I'd feared. I'm sorry for him, want to look after him. I'm fond of him. I *like* him. I guess . . . if all that means I love him . . . then I do love him. Unstructured and unsure though he is, with little to offer anybody."

"You're Americans. So, if he's with you, he doesn't have the problems of how to stay with a British lover —immigration, citizenship, work permits, so on—and he can go back to California where he can get a job and where his roots are . . . Roots *are* important, even at his age . . . You can give him a home, money, and security. Safe sex—"

"He uses contraceptives. If he didn't, I wouldn't allow him to do anything."

"I didn't mean in the Terrence Higgins sense. I meant psychologically safe. And he can lick cunt." She looked startled, indeed angry; I said, "He told me that."

"He told *me* he very much missed your cock."

I smiled. "I still have one, and he's welcome to it whenever he wants it. But we're getting off the point I was trying to make . . . the fact that you're Americans, and he doesn't therefore have any worries about a job or uprooting himself if he stays with you . . . and the security . . . isn't he just being selfish? Using you? I don't think he loves you, any more than he loves me. He's so . . . empty . . . he hasn't got any love to offer anyone."

"That's not quite fair."

"True, though."

"Of course, I've wondered about all that, but—"

I laughed, but not with any mirth. "I don't really see him sitting on the deck of your California house, discussing your biography of Chekhov. Making a dozen insightful points."

"I wouldn't dream of asking him to—"

"I think I'm going to tell him to fuck off out of my life."

"Don't do that." She touched my arm.

"Why not?" I thought of Simon. I didn't really know Simon at all, just had a few impressions of a person. But the man's *un*selfishness was so clear: the compassion, the sympathy, the—yes—love he had already shown me. Compared with the void at the centre of Kim! That patronising "You'll find somebody else quite easily," that arrogant "I love you, but not enough to live with you." The lack of compassion. "I'm going to tell him to fuck off," I repeated. "If you want to put up with being used, then you're welcome. I think you're a fool, if I may say so without being too offensive. You'll regret it in the end, I'm sure of that. Someone like Kim . . . he'll inevitably let you down."

"Hard words," she said. "Harsh words. I could say they're valid, to the point . . . I know the odds against him and me having a great deal of permanence are high. Though HIV"—she shrugged her shoulders—"may hold us together."

"I thought that once. Didn't work, Katya. And what if he gets ill?"

"Then I'll look after him."

"So . . . why shouldn't I tell him to fuck off?"

"Because he'll be devastated. He can't cope. And you can."

"I'm sorry," I said, "but that's his funeral."

"He needs the *two* of us! He likes men; have you forgotten? I can't satisfy all his needs . . . he's more homo than hetero! You know it! He still loves you. Wants you, cares about you. He said that . . . almost every day we were in Brittany!"

"This garbage about me coping better than him. I need the velvet glove treatment too! Prick me, and I also bleed! Can't you understand! Anyway . . . which did he prefer, Spain or Brittany?"

"He liked both."

"I mean as an experience."

"I wasn't with you in Spain," Katya said. "So how should I know? But he talked about it an immense amount! Not just the things seen, but the being with you . . . making love in the Manuel de Falla and on the tower at Zahara, how superb that was . . . the aeroplane in Castile . . . stork talk at Plasencia . . . Toledo's synagogue . . . the red hats like poppies . . . Señora Whatever-her-name-was and her Commie friends . . . sitting under the palm tree in the Generalife . . . so forth and so on!"

"All the high points. All the great memories. What he terms 'for evers'. How many were there in Brittany? Making love at Quimper, for example? Chatting up peasants in phrase-book Breton at Guimiliau? Poppies at Dinard? Prehistoric stones at Carnac? The church at Locronan? A café, as peculiar as the aeroplane, at Guingamp? Sitting under a storm-tortured tree, with a distant prospect of the Île de Sein or the Île d'Ouessant?" (Our boat to Spain had passed by Ushant, and we'd had a distant prospect from the far side. Did he remember as he looked, miss me when they made love—as he'd said of her when *we* made love?)

"He still cares about you," she repeated, thus side-stepping my question.

"He only cares about himself." I stood up. "I don't exist to pander to his need for male arsehole. I'm more than somewhere for him to park his cock. I deserve better!"

"Pride?"

"Yes. And why not? I'm proud I'm proud! I'm not here to be wiped on, like loo paper! I won't be second best!" I looked at my watch. "I have classes to teach. Goodbye, Katya."

She came to the door. "What sort of goodbye is this?" she asked.

"You mean just the usual au revoir, or is it really goodbye? I guess . . . you and I are much too old to quarrel, and I've known you much too long to smash up something we both value immensely. We aren't severers, anyway; are we? Too much good rich milk of human kindness—do I mean humankind-ness?—has flowed under the particular bridge you and I built. So it's au revoir, I'm sure. But I don't think I'll see you quite so often as of late . . . unless it's just you and me alone . . . not with *him*. Call me if it's an emergency . . . but otherwise I'll call *you*. I love you, Katya."

"I love you too." We kissed: most of the old affection was still there.

"I'm glad we're unable to quarrel," I said.

"So am I, Jesus God! But what will you do with your life now?"

"Oh . . . I don't know . . . I have an iron in the fire. And fire in my iron."

« NINE »

Mike and Danny were in a state of great excitement. After months of trying to get himself a teaching job somewhere, anywhere, and only receiving answers that said, "We regret to inform you that the post has been filled," Danny was on the short list for a job in the Drama department of a comprehensive school at Stowmarket in Suffolk. By an extraordinary stroke of luck, the school was also advertising for an experienced teacher of French; Mike had applied, and had been short-listed too. Their interviews were on the same day.

"If we're both successful," Danny said, "we're going to buy a cottage in the country. We've seen the one we want! We went up to Stowmarket last week-end just to look around . . . and we saw it. Exactly what we'd both like! It needs a lot of modernisation . . . gutting inside, really. But it's cheap, and if we work at it over the years, it could be tremendous! It doesn't have honeysuckle and

red roses round the door—yet!—but it has a big garden. I
enjoy gardening. I . . . of course I shouldn't be so enthusiastic—"

"Because we may not get the jobs," Mike said.

"Suppose one of you does and the other doesn't?" I
asked.

"Then I think we'll fuck off out of here and buy it; I
can just about raise the deposit for a mortgage. And
Danny's parents said they'll help."

"Oh." I didn't know quite what to say, so I resorted
to various conventional expressions of good wishes; "I
hope it all works out for you," and "Best of luck!"

"You'll have to find another shiatsu man," Danny
said.

I'd come for a shiatsu session now, and hadn't
thought Mike would be there. "Yes, I suppose I will," I said.

"We must stop counting chickens," Mike said.
"We'll be very upset if we don't succeed; so it would be
sensible to persuade ourselves that we won't. Then we
can be overjoyed if we do! But it's impossible not to plan
. . . to dream . . . we've already looked at colour charts
and curtain materials, talked about knocking the two
downstairs rooms into one . . . and rebuilding the bathroom. It's silly . . . but there we are. The first thing for
him to do is to buy some clothes for the interview. He
doesn't own a suit! Well . . . I'll leave you now. I'm off
to the library."

Danny said, when he had gone, "You know he writes
poetry? He wrote a poem for me the other day." He
seemed embarrassed, as if he was admitting to something

that should have remained private. His grin was shy and awkward.

"Do you want me to . . . to read it?"

"I . . . mmm . . . why not?" He went over to his desk, picked up a piece of paper, and handed it to me. The poem was called *Owls*.

> If you should make owls
>   I will not let their hard sour pellets
>   Churn in my stomach, spawning worms
> Of indigestion
>
> But spit them out
>   So that they die at once, just as
>   Unwanted seeds in fruit are spat
> To wither quickly.
>
> If I should make owls
>   Don't splinter me like shivered glass
>   Or tear the shared September silence
> To rags of Babel
>
> Smothering love
>   In me, creating ice—instead
>   Summon the meadowsweet and kingcups
> The blossom in me.
>
> Don't frighten me.
>   And if I do not anger you
>   Then owls' eggs will not hatch; pellets
> Will melt like sweets.

I'd seen it before. It had never been published, but it wasn't written for Danny; Mike had written it for his first lover, the man he'd lived with for ten years. Perhaps the weight of guilt about HIV was drying up his inspiration—I don't know, but it was odd that Danny had to make do with verses created for someone else; odder still that Mike should have to pretend it was new and specially for him. When first we practise to deceive, etcetera . . . This whole relationship is built on lies, I said to myself; it's *riddled* with lies. Yet the irony was that if the secrets could be successfully shrouded, it might work. As it would have done in Ibsen's *Wild Duck* if Gregers had not told the truth. No one was likely to tell the truth in this case; I wasn't Gregers, the thirteenth at dinner. But what had I got for being honest, in my own life, since HIV? Not much. The faint chance of Simon. And self-respect. Self-respect, however, didn't necessarily lead to fulfilment and joy.

"What do you think of it?" Danny asked.

"It's good. I hope you're flattered."

"I'm very flattered."

It wasn't particularly good. Mike's best work—the published stuff—was all concerned with the bitter break-up he'd experienced before I met him, poems in which anger and distress almost leaped at you off the page. This poem was not more than quite nice. I remembered some of the lines in the other poems, the strong and sinewy words:

> You told me in mid-winter. Another
> Christmas alone! How well you always
> Ruined Christmases! Almost sadistically,
> One in two, as regular as clockwork.
> Each spoiled season meant a new house. I think
> You'll always be remembered as the man

Who loved to decorate his boyfriends' rooms,
Then left.

"Shall we get on with the shiatsu?" I said.

It was good today. I fell asleep, and when I woke, I was tranquil, healed, at rest. Danny was becoming expert, strong and sinewy like the words I'd recalled. Reliable. He cradled my head as usual, then broke the silence: "That was the best session we've had in weeks. Whatever those problems were . . . they're going. You're much more in tune with your whole body." He bent down and kissed me. Stroked my face. He may be madly in love with Mike, I said to myself, but no doubt of one thing: he fancies me. I stir him. What could come of it . . . if I opened it up?

On another tack I said, "Do you and Mike have safe sex?"

"What's safe sex?"

"Fucking with condoms. Not coming in each other's mouths."

He stared at me. "Why on earth should we want to do that?"

A week after he returned from Brittany, Kim arrived at Stoke Newington. "I need you both," he said. I should have made him leave at once, but I couldn't bring myself to do it. I still loved him. Besides, I was curious. I wanted to see if he could explain his actions, to know what he would do next.

He kissed me several times, but they were dry kisses, lip on lip. I found it insulting, though he may not have thought so; he may simply have been thinking he should protect himself. From what? He already had the antibodies. Eventually I told him to stop. "I don't suppose you kiss *her* in that way. Do you?"

"No. But you and I have to be sure we don't pass our viruses back and forth to each other. Be infected by a different strain."

"Balls." Kissing was very low risk, the leaflet had said. Perhaps this new ploy, the dry kiss, was another bit of his revenge against me for making him positive—I couldn't help thinking his whole behaviour, since the day I told him what had happened, was motivated by an obsession with what the virus could do to *him*. Not to me. Love for me had died that day. Love for me: it had never existed.

"I've stopped smoking," he said. "*And* drinking. My health, for the rest of my life, is going to be my first concern." I knew it was wise for anyone antibody positive not to get drunk every night, alcohol being an immune depressant; but to give it up altogether was absurd. And I couldn't see what difference smoking could make. It was bad for you, of course; that was obvious—but it would hardly twitch the HIV virus one way or another.

He wanted to go to bed with me. "Why?" I asked. "Whatever for? I'm nothing but a disease-bag in your opinion. You don't really want my body. Or my mind and my heart, for that matter—you don't even see I have such things. I'm a gigantic virus to you, aren't I? A human immunodeficiency virus clothed in man's flesh. Not a living, lovable *person*."

"David . . . don't rag me. I can't help freaking out. I just can't! Every time I hear the word AIDS, I feel physically *sick*! I can't bear jokes about it . . . I can't even stand people talking about it seriously . . . and it's everywhere, in the newspapers . . . the TV programmes . . . it puts me in a complete flat spin!"

In bed, I said that I wasn't worried if he fucked me without a condom, that I didn't think his strain of the virus would be so very different from my own (if indeed he had the virus at all; we only knew he'd produced antibodies to *my* virus). He seemed to think that was O.K.: and screwed me, unsheathed. I didn't enjoy it—dry kisses, and my cock untouched except by hand, were all I was allowed. Anyway, I was too angry. His selfishness and the inconsistencies in his thinking made it, for me, a prime example of sex without love. Throughout the whole twenty minutes of it I thought of Simon's unselfishness. And knew what I had to do now.

"Gee! That was just great!" he said.

"Kim . . . it was the last time." We were lying side by side under the duvet, not quite touching. I wanted to smoke, as we always did after making love, but in deference to his having stopped, I didn't.

"What do you mean, it was the last time? You aren't serious!"

"I am. I want you to pack all your things

and . . . go. We've no further use for each other. No
point, no purpose. This relationship is all washed up,
high and dry on the sand."

"I don't believe you. I do not believe what I'm hearing! You can't do this . . . to *me*! I won't go!"

I got out of bed and started to dress. "If you won't
pack your things, I'll do it for you." It's always easier to
get rid of an unsatisfactory lover when there's a prospective lover on the horizon; virtually impossible if there's
nobody. Maybe I was looking for too much from Simon,
but I couldn't help thinking of him as a prospective
lover. It was possible—probable—he'd back off; that
would surely be the advice anyone would give him . . .
You can't have sex with a sexual outcast, they'd say.
But . . . maybe he wouldn't. You see, Katya, I *can't*
cope, alone. HIV is bad enough without this man constantly eroding me, damaging my psyche, bruising my
ego, wounding my self-image. There's a point on the
downward spiral of hurt when you have to stop, when
some little tremor of pride has to be encouraged (I'm
proud I'm proud, I'd said), because a further descent is
suicide—metaphorical or literal, as the case may be. If
Kim didn't get out of my life, I'd be smashed to bits.

I began to pull his tee-shirts and socks out of the
chest of drawers. "You leave those alone!" he shouted,
and, throwing off the duvet, he ran across the room, and
shoved me out of the way. He began to pack. Then
stopped, aware I was looking at him. And turned. The
most beautiful body I'd ever seen: the curves under the
pectorals, the light dusting of gold hair on his skin,

the big muscles. The fit, well-defined legs, the golden pubic hair, the excellently proportioned cock. Blue eyes, full mouth; golden curly hair. Michelangelo model. He threw his arms round me. "I didn't want this to happen," he said. "I didn't want it to end like this!" He was in tears.

"Nor did I. Please believe that. But . . . sometimes . . . there's no point in even trying to carry on."

"But I love you!"

"I love you too. As you said in Spain . . . it isn't enough."

I went downstairs, poured myself a stiff vodka and orange, and sat in my garden—the postage stamp Kim had named it, referring to its minute size. November now, but the high walls protected it so well it was possible to sit out here on many days in winter. Eventually, he came down from the bedroom; I heard him use the telephone. Then he helped himself to something from the fridge.

He came outside with a glass of milk, and said, "Do you want yours freshened?"

"No thanks."

"Mmm . . . I'm ready to go . . . Will you drive me to Islington? Katya's expecting me. I've just called her . . . and told her what's happened."

"Of course I will. You're moving in . . . permanently?"

"Yes. Until she's finished her book. After that, we'll go back to California together. David . . . if only I'd been able to explain . . . my fears to you . . . then . . . we might . . . "

I made no attempt to contact him, or Katya, for several weeks, and from their end of the telephone the silence was deafening. The most interesting events of November were the times I spent with Simon, with people from Body Positive, and the conversation I had at the hospital when I went for another blood test. Simon said he couldn't make love with me again, at least not yet: he had to have more breathing-space to come to the right decision about what, he now knew, was a momentous step—if, or when, we did so, it would be the start of a relationship to which he'd give everything: it would be a way of signifying that though I might have HIV, he'd take the risk because he loved me so much. All this pre-planning was understandable, but it made me uneasy. I was used to the idea of a relationship, whether it had begun with a night in bed or not, just growing naturally, so imperceptibly that you didn't notice it at first. This had happened with me and Kim; I got to a point when I said to myself this *is* a relationship, or it could be, and then did something about it. I didn't like the prospect of a visible Rubicon, the thought of a tricky examination, as it were, looming ahead.

We should spend our time together he said, just learning about each other. We met at week-ends, and two or three evenings during the week, and did all the usual things lovers might do, apart from jumping into the sack. In other words what we did was not important; it was the quality of the occasions that counted: the things discussed or not discussed, our reactions to each other and the outside world, the pleasure and enjoyment that demanded more pleasure and enjoyment. It was pretty good—the Shostakovich concert at the Festival Hall, the less than marvellous (we both thought) *King Lear* at the National Theatre, the nights in front of the TV or looking at photograph albums and playing silly games, dinner in restaurants, the trips into the country (Essex marshes, Surrey hills, cathedrals in Chichester and Rochester, the long, long kiss in the north transept of Winchester), dancing at the Hippodrome until four a.m., another long, long kiss as the sun rose over London. The usual activities, the normal syndromes of lovers.

Was I in love with him; did I love him? He me? I was slow to admit it to myself, in a way resisted the idea: I knew I could simply be bowled over with gratitude—someone was (unbelievably) showing an interest in a sexual outcast. Also, it was so near in time to my relationship with Kim; I wasn't a person who, as a rule, switched affections at the drop of a hat. Months, even years, had in the past occurred between relationships—bruises that needed to heal. HIV was turning my whole emotional self, the stability painfully acquired over two decades of adult living, upside down. I felt quite unable to trust my feelings, to use experience as a yardstick; I was unsure of what I really thought or felt about anything.

But I was sure I was discovering—uncovering—a very nice person. Mature, balanced, with a sense of humour like my own, and similar interests. I just kept wishing I was not HIV positive. But would it have made for any great difference, apart from having a sex life together? I couldn't know. On the other hand, I said to myself as I gave him a red rose one evening, I had long been thinking, before Kim, before I'd ever heard of AIDS, that courtship and wooing were marvellous activities gay liberation had been utterly stupid to throw out of the window. That time in the seventies and early eighties, when you met a man, ripped his knickers off, fucked, and then decided at breakfast whether the fucking meant you wanted to see him again, demeaned us to no more than our bodies, and often to just one part of them; conclusions were based solely on whether cock was efficient.

Saturday December the first. We wouldn't meet in the morning, he'd said, because he had things to do—cleaning his flat and taking his dirty clothes to the launderette. He came to my house in the afternoon, at ten to three, and, standing in the hallway, he took off his coat, his sweater, and his tee-shirt. Then his shoes and socks. "What the hell are you doing?" I asked. He didn't answer. He unzipped his jeans, pulled them down, stepped out of them.

Naked. "Carry me to bed. I've decided."

"But I don't have a condom."

"Oh!" He grabbed his jeans and held them in front of himself, as if acutely embarrassed—caught without clothes in the wrong place.

I started to giggle, and so did he; so much that we ended up on the floor in each other's arms, laughing helplessly. "I'll go out now and buy some," I said, when I'd recovered.

"It would seem . . . like a good idea."

"How many shall I get?"

"A gross." I must have looked surprised, for he

added, "I mean it."

"I love you," I said, kissing him. "I'll love you always. Care for you and keep you. You are a marvel!"

"And I'll care for you. Keep you. Love *you* always. *You* are a marvel."

"Warm the bed. I won't be long."

I'm not sure I'd ever felt as elated as I did that afternoon, driving away from my house to look for a gross of contraceptives. No other man, also HIV positive, I said to myself, could be so fortunate. December the first. A day I'd never forget.

« TEN »

I had good reasons, many good reasons, for saying no
other man could be so fortunate, some of which were
learned from the people I met through Body Positive. This
organization differed from the Terrence Higgins Trust in
that its primary concerns were the social needs of HIV
victims, though it also had its counsellors and worked
with AIDS patients in hospitals or in their homes, offering
support and friendship, and looking after their everyday
requirements. Its members met in pubs and in people's
houses; there were discussion groups, self-awareness
sessions, a disco every fortnight—something was happening most evenings of the week. It was very London-
oriented. It couldn't help but be so; most gay men with
HIV lived in the capital. Branches of Body Positive existed elsewhere, but lack of numbers—not perhaps numbers of people with the virus, but those who knew they
had it and were willing to share that knowledge—meant
provincial groups were very thin on the ground. Quite a

few men I met through Body Positive had moved to London simply because they had HIV: living in rural England, they felt, would lead to the death of their emotional and sexual selves.

I didn't want the counselling, I decided; I was more interested in meeting others like me and hearing their stories. Originally, I'd hoped to find a man I'd be attracted to, have sex with, form a relationship with, but that was pre-Simon. Simon had removed the problem. He is a saint, I said to myself, and was again uneasy: my position, as a man with the virus, was distorting my judgments.

The counselling would certainly have helped when I first knew, but though I'd heard of Body Positive then, and had some of their literature, I was in too much distress about Kim to think clearly. Counselling would have helped us both, but no one at the hospital pointed us in the right direction. I felt I had now come to terms with HIV and didn't require therapy. Yes, I'd wondered how long it would be before the virus destroyed my immune system, and which opportunistic disease would bring me to a protracted and awful death; were my insurances in order and my will: but perhaps it's age, experience of life, or the cast of mind of each particular individual—I wasn't a worrier. I was, from the beginning, reassured by learning that most people who had the virus did not develop AIDS. I was going, for once, to be part of a majority, I told myself. Many possible factors might be the cause of the virus attacking some men and women and not others—syphilis and hepatitis damaging the immune

system. And stress. You could torment yourself into getting AIDS. The only thing to do was to carry on with the
next job—teaching, giving a dinner party, putting the
postage-stamp garden to bed for the winter. Kim, of
course, had not helped to alleviate my stress, but Simon
had: Simon healed.

I was surprised to discover that many people in Body
Positive were unable to come to terms as quickly as I had.
They appeared, often, to have done so; they were serene,
or fairly content, but when they talked about their sex
lives, they showed themselves as far from well. HIV was
an immense kick at their libidos: they had lost their desire for sex, couldn't see themselves any longer as sexual
beings, and they seemed to take this as something they
had to live with, if only temporarily—though temporarily
might be months or years. This hadn't happened to me. I
wasn't damaged in desire or function. I felt almost guilty,
indeed irresponsible; maybe this *should* have happened
to me: it was as if I'd not taken the problem seriously
enough. But that was stupid, I told myself; I should count
my blessings.

Not everyone was like this. There were men who
were sexually active, and a fortunate few who had found
lovers by going to a Body Positive meeting. The one thing,
however, most people wanted to do was talk, to share
their own experiences, be listened to, be comforted. The
disco was the oddest I'd ever attended—almost nobody
came for the dancing. It was certainly the friendliest; it
reminded me of the spirit of comradeship and solidarity
that flourished in the early days of gay liberation. In fact,

the whole business of HIV was like a second coming out: you thought it over, accepted it (or not, as the case might be), began to do something about it—which people did you tell; who could be trusted with the knowledge?

There were men whose story was similar to mine—their lovers had panicked, been furious or devastated, had deserted them; though in every single instance, the lover had been antibody negative. When both partners had tested positive, they had grown closer together. No one had heard of behaviour like Kim's—proving to be positive, then rushing off to a lover who was not—and they were unanimous in condemning his actions as totally irresponsible. Ironically, I found I was defending him: I did, I think, know him and could see why he'd done what he did. Condemnation of Mike, when I talked about him and Danny, was just as strong, though behaviour like Mike's was not unprecedented. There were stories too, of people being dismissed from their jobs when employers had heard of their condition, or being thrown out of the places where they lived by landlords or lovers who seemed to think AIDS could be caught from door-knobs or coffee-cups or lavatory seats. And of people who were unwell in small ways—constantly tired, or their glands were swollen; their skin itched, or they couldn't easily throw off coughs, colds, or flu.

I met a man who had Kaposi's sarcoma; he'd been given two years, at most, to live. It was the first time I'd seen the distinctive and unsightly purple blotches; at least I'd now know what it was, I said to myself, if I was ever a victim. He was a cheerful and amusing character, about my age. He'd accepted the death sentence, he told me, and was determined to enjoy himself while he still could. He'd recently been in hospital, but had recovered enough to be discharged for the moment; and he'd felt sufficiently well that evening to venture out and chat to people over a few pints of beer. I didn't say so, but I thought, as I did of Simon, that he was a marvel, a revelation. If one thing impressed me more than anything else about some of the men I met through Body Positive, it was their courage, their sheer *goodness*. I was in grave danger, I realised, of beginning to view the world as morally black and white, not the complex shades of grey in which I generally saw it. But, I said to myself, the decision to be a part of Body Positive was a decision *not* to behave as Kim and Mike had done; it was another Rubicon, in this case a line that separated sheep from goats. Naive of me. There were doubtless plenty of moral failings in these men; those who appeared to be virtuous and were not, who may well have publicly proclaimed their intentions of never passing the virus to someone who was antibody negative, and in private—through meeting sexual contacts in all the usual ways—went on doing so regardless. But I wasn't aware of it.

Simon was often with me on these occasions; he needed, he said, to know as much as he could about the problem, and also—he admitted this a bit shamefacedly —to see men with the virus as functioning, normal human beings, not just statistics in a magazine article on

AIDS, or the monsters they were suggested to be in *The Sun*. And he came with me too when I went to the hospital for another blood test.

A routine check, to see if my immune system—the lymphocyte count was of particular importance—remained intact. The S.T.D. adviser was not there, so I asked Dr Marion if all gay men were still being told they should take the test. He smiled, then said, "We're sending them away to think about it first. Talk to their friends . . . and so on. Why?"

"Because it's useless, isn't it? All you learn is whether you've been exposed to the virus. You don't know how badly . . . or if you'll get AIDS or not . . . it doesn't lead to a cure . . . it just gives one piece of information which is *shattering* to the person concerned. It's totally destructive . . . it breakes up relationships . . . it's led to suicides."

He nodded. "So we're beginning to use a bit more caution."

"Why isn't there any proper counselling in the hospitals?" I asked. "People should be told before they take the test what the psychological damage is likely to be. And helped afterwards to come to terms with it."

"Because there's no funding. A few hospitals—a *very* few—are able to employ full-time or part-time counsellors, but we get nothing at all from the Department of Health to pay for it. We're sending people to Body Positive, Terrence Higgins—"

"Why didn't you tell *me* that?"

"We didn't realise, then, what the problems would be."

"You should have done. I have—"

"Listen. This is one of the most deadly viruses the world has ever seen, and if we think we've got problems now, we're also aware that in a few years' time the cases will have trebled, quadrupled . . . it could be of epidemic proportions. And it won't just be gay men. I wouldn't be surprised if, even now, something like fifty per cent of this country's haemophiliacs have the virus. We must use whatever we can to try and stop its spread. The test is far from perfect, a very blunt instrument . . . but if it means that people who would otherwise be infected avoid that infection, then . . . I think we have no option but to go on using it."

"Weigh that up against the vast amounts of misery it's caused."

"I know." He looked at his watch. "I'm very busy, but—"

I stood. "O.K.," I said in disgust. "I get the message; I've had my few minutes."

"I didn't mean that at all! Sit down." I hesitated. "What I was going to say is tell me what's on your mind. What's happened to *you* as a result of finding yourself positive. I seem to work twenty-five out of twenty-four hours a day now . . . all the extra work is counselling I'm not trained for. Do you know, I was sent off last

month on a crash mini-course . . . it's the only training
I've ever had. You can imagine what use *that* is! But I
am . . . trying."

I was surprised. I started to look at him not as a doctor, but as a human being. It was the first time I'd ever
looked at *any* doctor as a human being; not one I'd con-
sulted in the past had invited such an intrusion—their
concern was solely with symptoms, reaching for their
pads to write out a prescription (often before I'd finished
telling them what was wrong), and getting rid of me as
quickly as possible. So he heard the story of Kim, and
Katya; Simon; Mike and Danny. He asked if Simon had
come with me, and when I said he was waiting outside, he
told me to fetch him in. There was no particular point in
doing that, medically speaking, but I was glad he'd
suggested it, and I felt proud, sitting in that little
office—so minute it had room only for the three of us, and
the desk with my documents all marked "High Risk"—
holding hands with Simon, so that Dr Marion could for
once see gay love, not just the diseases gays brought to
him.

"Maybe your friend Danny should come in and take
the test," he said.

This disheartened me: I felt that I'd got nowhere at
all, that he'd learned nothing. "What on earth good
would it do?" I said, crossly. "Let him go on being ignorant! Being happy!"

"But suppose he has sex with somebody who's not
his lover?"

"He won't."

Dr Marion heaved a great sigh, then yawned. "Oh God! I'm weary! I'm not sleeping well . . . I have to admit, in moments in the small hours, I've thought that apart from checking blood supplies we should stop this test. One of the suicides . . . he was a patient I'd seen two months ago."

"I'm sorry."

"Do you think David will get AIDS?" Simon asked. "Do you think I will?"

"You? Have you had a test?"

"No," Simon said. "And I don't intend to."

"You know what precautions to take, I imagine. The risk is splitting the condom . . . do be careful! No violent thrusting . . . be gentle. And he should come out afterwards as quickly as possible." Dr Marion had worked out which way we preferred to be in bed. "If he goes limp and the condom comes off . . . "

Simon smiled. "I like him to be gentle."

"Will David get AIDS? I don't know, do I? There's an excellent chance he will not." He looked at my documents. "At the moment his immune system is better than mine. Two point seven lymphocyte count in September . . . that's good . . . no reason to think today's count should be less. We'll know in a fortnight."

"What's wrong with your immune system?" I asked.

He had an allergy to wheat germ, he explained; certain foods could kill him. For the next fifteen minutes he talked about himself, his wife, and his children. He hoped, he said, he was devoid of any prejudice against gays—he'd seen thousands in his work as a venerealogist and had never disliked one of us. We wouldn't have guessed, he added, that he was a practising Christian, and these past twelve years a churchwarden.

"Are you?" I said, not quite knowing how to respond to that.

He looked at his watch again. "I really must see the next patient," he said. "Simple case of the pox . . . hah! Simple! It seems so, compared with AIDS . . . come back in four months' time, sooner if you think anything's wrong."

"We're in good hands," Simon said, when we were out in the street.

"We?"

"We're in this together, David. There are no escape clauses."

"I . . . I really don't deserve . . . "

"But we *do* deserve each other. In *my* opinion."

"I just wish . . . I wish . . . Dr Marion had thought a few months back as he thinks now."

"Meaning you wouldn't have taken the test if he'd been able to say then what he said today?"

"I suppose."

"*Not* good thinking. Very poor thinking! If that had happened, you'd be worried for ever; did Mike give it to you, or didn't he give it to you? And you'd still be with Kim. I won't ask which you prefer, Kim or me, because I know the answer."

"You gorgeous, sweet man! I'm going to kiss you." Which I did, right by a bus stop, much to the astonishment and disapproval of a fat, middle-aged woman in a fur coat, and her lean, thin-faced friend.

"I've seen it all now, May," the fat woman said, as she stepped onto a 73 bus.

Christmas. I had no living relatives, apart from a cousin in Australia—it was he, the inheritor of all my property, I was thinking of when I was worrying about my will—so Christmas was usually spent with friends or lovers. On the whole I thought I was more fortunate than most, not having to devote the winter solstice to people I mightn't care for much, but occasionally I felt a big, Dickensian family Christmas would be fun. This year I got my wish—Simon took me to his parents' house in Norwich. The days were filled with aunts, uncles, grandparents, cousins, brothers, sisters, nephews and nieces; enormous meals and too much alcohol; presents, silly games, paper hats, crackers, cigar smoke, warmth and friendliness. Simon's parents, who appeared to have no hangups of any sort about homosexuality, didn't in the least mind him bringing to their Christmas celebrations a male lover they'd never seen (though they'd heard of me from letters and phone calls), nor did they disapprove of us sleeping in the same bed. It was all regarded as perfectly normal, though nothing was mentioned in front of the various aunts and uncles, etcetera. "This is Simon's friend," was how I was introduced. I enjoyed myself hugely. I hadn't had such a Christmas since I was a child.

A week beforehand, I posted, along with all my other Christmas mail, a card each to Katya and Kim—

"from David and Simon with love." This, I thought, would make Katya sufficiently curious to phone me: I had to speak to her—I couldn't allow Christmas to pass without talking to the woman I'd considered till recently my closest friend—but I was reluctant to make the first move. She rang on the day before Christmas Eve, and of course wanted to know who Simon was. I told her, and she said she hoped I was happy. She sounded relieved, as if a weight of guilt had been lifted.

"How's Kim?" I asked.

"O.K. Coming to terms. He says he needs a period of calm."

"Is he getting it?"

"He's here. Do you want to talk to him?"

"I'm not sure." My heart was beginning to race. "How are you both? As a couple, I mean."

"Oh, fine. Just fine."

There was a long pause. "Well, I guess I'll see you in the New Year," I said.

"I'd like that. Shall we go out to dinner? Just the two of us."

"Phone me and we'll make a date. Katya . . . no presents this Christmas. All right?"

"If . . . that's what you want." (We'd exchanged presents for at least a decade however far apart in the world we were; this year, ironically, we were about two miles from each other.) "We're having a quiet Christmas," she said. "Just the two of us, but Steve and Anne fly in on the twenty-seventh, so I guess there'll be some partying then." Steve was her eldest son, Anne his live-in girlfriend. "Here's Kim."

No chance, then, to make up my mind about wheth-er I wanted to talk to him or not. "I miss you," he said. "I . . . don't feel . . . we deserved to lose each other." I didn't know what to say. "Are you there, David?"

"Yes."

"I walk about London . . . and think of all the things we did. The places you showed me. It hurts. Sometimes . . . it's *agony.* I still love you. Not enough, maybe . . . but I've said that before, I guess. You shouldn't have sent me away, do you hear? You should have given me time . . . you should have listened to me . . . Who is this Simon? Is he important?"

"Yes."

"Does he live with you?"

"No."

"Is he a great fuck?"

A long silence. "We shouldn't be talking like this," I said.

"Is he better in bed than me?"

"No. Not better. Just . . . different."

"How, different?"

"I'm not going to discuss it."

"I miss you," he said again. "Shall we get together some time? Just the two of us. I'd like that."

"What would be the point?"

"I'm . . . not sure. Do you think it's a good idea?"

Another long silence. "No," I said.

"I'm in therapy now. I go to this guy . . . once a week. I don't have to pay. Thank God you have a free health plan here! He's cute, and nice." He giggled. "I guess I could fall in love with him."

"Perhaps . . . you fall in love too easily. Or think you do."

"No. No, that's not so. I was joking. I love you . . . only you. And Katya."

"Two into one won't work," I said.

"I don't see why not. It happens."

"Sure it happens. But not for you with me. It's too selfish. And painful. It's . . . just wanting the good times. Not putting anything back in. No commitment."

"Like a prostitute, you mean?"

"I didn't say so."

Our third immense silence. "I guess I'd better hang up now," he said.

"Have a good Christmas. Give my love to Steve and Anne. I haven't seen them since . . . oh, before I ever met you! How time flies!"

"I'll talk to you again, in the New Year."

I said: "Maybe."

« ELEVEN »

The last shiatsu. All Danny's and Mike's dreams were coming true: they'd succeeded in getting the jobs at Stowmarket, and they were buying their cottage. The appointments at the school began in January, so they were moving to Suffolk in two days' time, the fifth of the month. "I can't believe our luck!" Danny said. "I really can't! Something is sure to go dreadfully wrong."

"I don't see why." I looked round: nearly everything was packed, in boxes and crates and cartons. Sadness: the feeling was always present in rooms that were losing their owners—I was aware, in a way I wasn't before, of dust and cobwebs, holes in walls where screws had once supported bookshelves, white squares where pictures had hung, forlorn cracks in the plaster.

"I think you're allowed only a certain quantity of luck." The superstitious side of Danny: I asked myself, not for the first time, if shiatsu was merely primitive mumbo-jumbo, enjoyable and salutary though I found it.

All that yin and yang, pressure points and meridians he believed in; was it more credible than astrology or palm reading, or those ancient folk-tales that finished with the hearer being told he would have seven years' good fortune and win every time in battle? No more credible, I guess; it depended for its effect, as many things did—relationships, for example—on faith and trust.

I lay on the floor. "We all need to express ourselves through body contact with other human beings," Danny said. (He could be sententious at times.) "Often, we satisfy this need through sex, but the desire for sex can get in the way of warmth and love, can spoil things. Shiatsu helps us to be in touch with our intuitive feelings for one another."

Today, he was at his best—confident, gentle, and authoritative. Every movement of his fingers was pleasant, whether it was on the arms, the legs or the stomach. Did I enjoy it, I asked myself yet again, because he was so very cute; were his warm hands, sweating a little (despite the freezing winter weather outside), so welcome because I'd like to touch with my hands too, and our mouths: have the freedom to caress his skin, experience a more overtly sexual stimulation? Perhaps. But not wholly so. If the sensation was just erotic, I couldn't do what I did now—fall asleep as I lay on my back, Danny working slowly on my neck and the upper part of my arms.

And dreamed: he was working slowly on my cock. I woke gradually, and thought I was still dreaming—but my jeans were unzipped, and my cock, very erect, protruded above my knickers. The warm, sweaty hand was wrapped round it. "What the hell are you doing?" I said.

"The shiatsu is finished, and God knows when I'll see you again. We've always wanted this, both of us. There may never be another opportunity."

He moved, so he was on his knees, one leg either side of my body. He bent down, and began to suck. I shivered: the pleasure was intense. "Will you tell Mike?" I asked.

"No."

He lifted me, and pulled my jeans down, pulled them right off. (I wasn't wearing shoes; one never did during shiatsu.) I didn't stop him. But I asked myself some important questions, as his fingers travelled up under my shirt and stroked my nipples. Would I tell Simon? Did Simon ever do this with another man? We'd not discussed it; we just assumed neither of us did, or would. That is what trust is. He lay down on me, began to kiss me. What if he suggested, indeed demanded, something more than safe sex; what should I say, and when, and how?

"Let's go to bed," he murmured.

Under the cool sheets, both of us naked, exploring. A new country. Sex in the afternoon—the skin is more responsive than at night; at least I find it so. Something to do with body rhythms, alertness, lack of alcohol. Our mouths, our tongues were deliciously sweet. I'd have difficulty holding it back if we didn't pause soon, and still it was safe sex, no hint that he wanted to enter me, or have me inside him. Perhaps I wouldn't need to say anything. But if I did, if I said I was HIV positive, he'd automatically wonder if Mike was; he knew we'd gone to bed in the past. To open up such a can of worms . . . it was almost as bad as *not* saying anything.

He reached for the KY. "I'm going to fuck you," he said.

"No."

"Why not? You want it. I know you want it."

"I don't think we should."

"That's absurd." He pushed my legs back, raised them onto his shoulders. Christ! How I longed for it! I couldn't resist . . . the beautiful body; the cock ready to penetrate.

"Do you have a condom?"

He looked surprised, and said, "Of course not. You asked me that once before. Why do you think I need such a thing?"

"I'm HIV positive." He seemed bewildered. "I took the test. I have the virus."

He jumped up and away from me, as if he'd put his hands on a revolting slimy object. Sexual outcast, I said to myself; that's me. How sad it all is, how fucking sordid! Grey, grey world. "When? How?" he asked. "Have you infected Mike? Jesus, if you've infected Mike . . . then I've got it too!" He scrambled off the bed; his cock slowly deflating, a sliver of pre-come dangling from it. A variety of expressions flitted over his face—hurt, betrayal, amazement: horror.

"No, I haven't infected Mike," I said. (Which was absolutely true.)

"Thank God for that! Jesus! When did you discover? Just recently?"

"Since . . . some time after . . . Kim arrived in England."

"So . . . he gave it to you?" He nodded, assuming this to be correct. "Well, it figures. He's an American." An absurd deduction, but not uncommon. He said, "I'm going to the loo."

When he returned, I said, "I'm sorry. Very sorry." I wasn't apologising for having HIV (something I felt no need to be apologetic about), but for giving him such a fright, and because I'd spoiled some very good sex.

"It's O.K." He started to put his clothes on. "I'm sorry for *you*. It must be awful."

"It . . . could be worse."

"I'm glad you told me. It must have been difficult . . . mmm . . . considering the situation we were in."

"Yes. I would have *loved* you to fuck me."

"I was dying for it! I am still!" The old mischievous grin, the full twinkle. "I was so turned on . . . so ready to shoot floods and *floods* . . . my balls ache!"

"We could . . . use our hands."

He shook his head. "Aching balls or not . . . I don't think so."

I pulled my jeans on. "At least we don't have anything on our consciences. We haven't screwed behind our lovers' backs."

He laughed. "How sophistical of you! We so nearly
did, I reckon it makes no difference. Do you have to exchange sperm to commit adultery?"

"Probably . . . not."

"Mike said, as we may not see you for I don't know
how long, do you want to meet him for a drink this evening? Nine o'clock in the King Edward the Sixth?"

"Yes . . . Where is he now?"

"Somewhere in Hornsey, hiring a van for moving day."

When I was dressed I said I'd better leave. He
didn't try to stop me: no elderflower or jasmine this afternoon. Maybe the tins were all packed in one of the crates.
When we parted, we always kissed, but as I touched him
now on the shoulders, and moved towards him, he didn't
bend his mouth towards mine, just offered his cheek.
However much I could make room for people's ignorance
and fear, it was still a slap. So I didn't kiss him. "Look
after yourself," he said. "I'll see you, no doubt. One of
these days."

Should I tell Simon, I wondered as I went home. I decided
not to. Sleeping dogs, hornets' nests, and so on. It obviously wouldn't happen again. Ten years ago, dizzy with
gay freedom and open relationships, I'd have thought it
quite wrong, very dishonest, to hide such a thing; in that
era of screwing around, it was an essential part of life to
inform your lover that you'd been with a trick. That, of
course, had its penalties as well as its rewards; distrust
and jealousy—despite what one heard of in other people's

lives—ensued more frequently than a greater trust, or admiration for honesty. I had once lost a lover, who only weeks after we met started to have sex again with his former affair: if he wanted to I should allow it, I reasoned. He wasn't doing it because of unbridled desire, or so I thought; it was simply affection, and it would be foolish of me to get angry and insecure. How naive I was! Three months later they were back together permanently. Maybe he thought I didn't love him very much, as I hadn't tried to stop them screwing. Or in those pre-AIDS days, when every imaginable permutation was indulged in, the first guy might have said: fine, I'll give you six months off while I do the same thing. Who knows? I was very hurt, but I got over it. I can't now remember what either of those two men looked like. So much for depth of feeling!

I was becoming a conservative in more ways than one: not only the elaborate courtship with Simon and the moral viewing of the world in colours more black and white than previously, but I had no inclination to be promiscuous, and as for adultery, it should, I'd discovered, be as secret as any such act in a Victorian melodrama. Was it HIV that had brought this about—or age? A bit of both, perhaps. I'd said to Kim that Simon and I weren't living together, which was true; but it was something we'd discussed a great deal. And that, it seemed, would turn out to be like an old-fashioned couple moving into their first home, a place looked for and acquired while we stayed in our separate establishments: for Simon had no wish to move into my house, nor I into his flat. We would buy somewhere, and jointly, half each; not till then would

I live with him. (But, unlike the old-fashioned couple, this did not preclude us sleeping together.) A house jointly owned: I had qualms. I had never experienced such an arrangement, had always valued the independence of being a sole proprietor, enjoyed closing the door, if I needed to, on the rest of the world. That more than one lover had lived in my house, on occasion for long periods of time, wasn't the same as joint ownership; there was always a hint of impermanence in a lodger or a tenant. It was the finality of the act that alarmed me; the commitment implied. Suppose we regretted it? It wouldn't be easy to cancel.

But the only way of finding out, I decided, was to get on and do it: as with nearly everything important, so much had to be taken on trust. It wasn't Simon I had doubts about; it was me. Was I—particularly after the episode in Danny's bed—to be trusted? Simon's belief in me was a source of joy, but it was also a serious responsibility. It had to be sustained, nurtured. I would do my best, I reassured myself, as I shut my mind on the scene with Danny, to devote my life to a man I knew much less well than, for example, Katya—whose recent behaviour I certainly could not have predicted, and I'd thought I'd have been able to predict anything about her.

Get on and do it, I said again; the only way to live.

Getting on and doing it at the moment was often concerned with introducing each other to our friends. It was perhaps easier for me, initially, to be accepted by his friends than for him to be clutched to the bosoms of mine. He had not had, for a long while before meeting me, anyone of great significance; his friends were delighted he now had such a person, and were therefore prepared to think well of me: if I was Simon's lover, I must be O.K. But my friends did not know what to make of my odd and inexplicable switch from one man to another; if they thought me strangely unsettled, they'd presumably think Simon would be so too. I wasn't able to tell them why Kim and I had split up, unless I also told them that I had HIV, and I didn't particularly want to do that. Maybe I would in my own good time and when I needed to, but not just because it illuminated another matter. Their comments were, as always, what I might have expected, Keith saying it was just as well he hadn't allowed his roses to go back to briar, and Tony convinced that Kim must have had an experience with a Breton onion-man far more earth-shattering than any I could produce. Chris said I couldn't have hoped, surely, to hold on to a guy as good-looking as Kim for more than ten minutes; but Dizzy and Maria were sympathetic and sad that Barbara Cartland with balls was not alive and well. One of the reasons why the two women were fond of Kim was that although he was so obviously "male", he was, as they saw it, very gentle; when the four of us were together we had often been two pairs—Kim and Dizzy, the "men" (we joked), and me and Maria. With Simon it was different. He disappeared to the kitchen with Maria to discuss recipes. It sounds like an awful piece of stereotyping, as if I was going on to say Dizzy and I were left in the lounge to drink beer in pint mugs. We weren't, but I did spend longer with her than when Kim was around. She asked few questions about

Simon, just said she hoped it would work. With Kim, she'd always demanded the details. She knew I hadn't told her the full story of why we'd broken up, and maybe she resented that. Not a lot I could do about it, however; as I said, I would tell her if and when I needed to.

Though I acted very decisively in making Kim leave, it wasn't characteristic; in the past, even when nothing was left in a relationship and it was beyond high time for them to move on, I'd allowed lovers to go of their own accord. Kim wasn't yet out of my system—another problem for me-and-Simon. When we made love, I sometimes lay there, thinking of Kim. Wishing it had been Kim. The absence of his smell, his gasps during orgasm, his uninhibited animality: I missed it all. What I missed most was that he'd never really given himself to me (though he pretended he had); he'd entered my world, examined it, liked it, enjoyed it—then discarded it. He'd never thought to stay as Simon, curled up against me, relaxed, satisfied, at peace, intended to stay. I loathed the failure that Kim represented. Missing him was perhaps selfishness: I wasn't good enough for him. I suppose we all want to think we are good enough for every man who comes into our lives. When we're not, there's an everlasting awareness of our own imperfection.

Much, much better, I told myself, to be good enough for Simon. I forced Kim out of my head, and slipping my arms round Simon, I stroked him, kissed the back of his neck. "I'll make it work," I said.

"You *are* making it work," he replied, sleepily.

"I hope so."

"What's the matter?"

"Nothing."

"Good."

"I love you."

Mike was so concerned to tell me about the successful job interviews and how the purchase of the cottage was going, that it was difficult to get him to react to what I wanted to say; but he did drift far enough from his own affairs to tell me that Paul had been taken to hospital again, with pneumocystis carinii: and was not responding favourably to the treatment. Robert had phoned with this information; since Mike had got together with Danny, Robert and Paul had been seeing a great deal of each other. "I haven't really had the time," Mike said, "to keep in touch with them the past few months."

"Do you ever think," I said, as I helped myself to an olive from the bowl the pub management had kindly left on the counter, "that you're opting out of your responsibilities?"

He looked guarded, even a bit frightened. "What do you mean?"

"Those of us with HIV shouldn't bury our heads in the sand and pretend it doesn't exist. Pretend the people with it don't exist. Aren't you living on borrowed time?"

He lit a cigarette, and puffed at it nervously. "Just as well I'm moving away from you; you're too uncomfortable! Like Hamlet's father's ghost. All right . . . say I *have* buried my head in the sand if you wish . . . it's true. I don't think about AIDS. I don't think about being positive. I haven't been for another blood test . . . I don't want to know! If it gets me . . . it gets me. I've scrubbed it out of my mind . . . to all intents and purposes, I've never had a test; I never had a result; there's nothing wrong with me."

"And what about Danny."

"What about Danny?"

"Why don't you tell him, even now? It's not too late."

He shook his head. "I can't."

"Why?"

"Because . . . I'm terrified of losing him." He ate an olive, thoughtfully.

Remembering Danny's reaction to what I'd told him that afternoon—leaping away as if he had been burned—this was possibly a reasonable deduction, but I said, "He's a nice guy. A mature guy. He loves you . . . he's thrown in his lot with you; you're going to bury yourselves—no, not in sand!—in a love nest in the country. Perhaps, on second thoughts, that *is* a way of burying yourself in the sand. He's a good person, Mike. I think he'd forgive you. But with every day that passes . . . telling him becomes less easy. How can you live with him and love him . . . *make* love with him . . . knowing what you may be doing to him? I can't even begin to imagine such a hell on earth!"

"David, I didn't want it to be like this! It just happened . . . in that hotel room in Cambridge! That first night. Everything I've done since then . . . or not done . . . has been dictated by that."

"What would you think of Paul if he'd screwed you *knowing* he had AIDS?"

"Can we move onto something else? This topic . . . is boring. And I don't see why I should be subjected to the third degree. Do you want another drink?"

"Yes."

He went to the bar, and returned with two more pints of lager. "Have you seen the new production of *Three Sisters*? Danny and I found it—"

"How's Robert? Has he had a test? Is he positive? Has he got AIDS?"

He looked very annoyed at my persisting with the previous conversation, but I didn't care. He sipped his lager. "He hasn't had a test. He hasn't any symptoms of . . . anything."

"This topic, as you call it—the word is hardly serious enough—is *not* boring. Maybe he should have a test . . . is he sleeping around? Giving it to others?"

"I didn't enquire about his sex life. I'm not my brother's keeper."

"Thus do germs multiply. The epidemic spreads. And at the risk of sounding pompous . . . I think people with HIV should *all* be their brother's keepers. Love one another or die."

"I love Danny."

"You call it love?"

I'd pushed him too far. "I don't see why I should have to stay here and listen to all this shit!" He banged his glass on the table.

"Go then," I said.

But he didn't. He was silent for a while, then he said, "How's *your* sex life?"

"I have one." I dipped into the olives again.

"Oh?"

"No further comment." 'Sex life', as a summing up of me-and-Simon, was about as unserious as 'topic' was to describe HIV. "How many other people have you told you're positive?" I asked.

"Nobody. The less said the better."

"Not even Robert?"

"No."

"Then why did you tell me?" There were two olives left; I took one of them.

"Ah." He smiled. "Perhaps I shouldn't say this, but . . . as we're unlikely to see each other again for a bit . . . and maybe I don't, come to think of it, want to see you again at all . . . I told you because . . . Did you never realise it, David? Never have an inkling?"

"Of what?"

"Well . . . sensitivity to others isn't your strong suit, I suppose."

"Get to the point, fuck you! Realise what?"

"That I'd long since come to the conclusion that, for me, *you* were in all likelihood Mr Right."

I stared at him, amazed. "And you said nothing! Not even when I'd thrown that glass bowl at Kim! When I fucked you as if it was the last fuck we'd ever have! And you said we shouldn't do anything for the wrong reason!"

"It was too late. You only had eyes for Kim. Anyway . . . I'd met Danny by then, and he *is* Mr Right."

"What's that got to do with telling me you were HIV positive?"

Again, the guarded, almost frightened look in his eyes. "I feel guilty about this . . . not so guilty, I admit, as keeping Danny in ignorance . . . but somewhat reprehensible. I thought it would break up your relationship with Kim. Then, having no one, you'd come to me . . . both of us antibody positive . . . and we'd—"

"Fall madly in love, and live happily ever after?" My stare wasn't amazed now, more one of withering contempt. "Psychologically a little . . . off-beam, wasn't it?"

He was trying to look anywhere other than at me. "I suppose so."

"If it alleviates your guilt just a fraction . . . I'll say this: I didn't have the test because you said I should. I'm too old to be influenced very much by other people telling me what I ought to do. I made up my own mind; it was my decision, and my decision alone. You needn't worry about it! As for using it to try and split lovers apart . . . well, it certainly succeeded! But what a way to go on . . . it's *disgusting*! You call it love? You think you loved me? You did it because you loved me?" He was silent. I grabbed his arm and twisted it. "You'll answer that if it's the last thing you do!" His beer went flying, spilling onto his jeans.

"Yes!" he shouted. "Now let go of me! I'm dripping wet!"

I released him, and he began to mop himself with his handkerchief. "I said Kim knew nothing about love, that all he was concerned with was selfish taking . . . but you . . . you know as much about love as this chair. You're an absolute pachyderm."

"Pachyderm?"

"Ungulates that do not ruminate. Pigs and elephants
—thick-skinned and insensitive. You told me just now
you didn't want to see me again. Frightened I'll whisper
something in Danny's ear? *I* certainly don't want to see
you again!" I took the last olive, got up and left. At the
door I shouted to him, "Ask Danny who was in your bed
this afternoon!"

I shouldn't have said that. I should *not* have said
that! It was evil. But said it I had.

I felt a sudden, enormous desire for Simon.

« TWELVE »

In March we moved into our new house. It was only three streets away from where I'd been living; I had no difficulty selling that property, despite—maybe even because of—the postage-stamp size of the garden. The one at the new house was much bigger, which pleased me, though it meant nothing to Simon, who was totally uninterested in gardening. He liked the results I produced, however; the flowers and shrubs. The weeks that followed the move were devoted to painting and wallpapering, arranging and re-arranging furniture, buying this or deciding there was no room for that. We quickly grew into being an almost sedentary couple, staying at home in the evenings to read, watch television and just live with each other; we hardly ever went out to a film or a play, or ventured into a pub or a disco, though we continued to have a social life with our friends. This new conservative self I'd found suited me. And Simon. My fears and worries about the relationship—the speed of it, the commitment, my putting him too much on a pedestal, seeing him as a saint—proved to be quite daft. We were both happy. It worked.

The spring and early summer passed without surprises. I didn't become ill—my status as an asymptomatic carrier was unaltered—and Dr Marion told me, each time I had my blood checked, that my lymphocyte count was better than his own. I didn't even catch a cold that dull, damp spring. Simon changed his mind about the test. Even though our love life was always "safe", he came with me and had himself tested whenever I went to the hospital. He was, each time, antibody negative.

Robert called me—he had got the number, he said, from Mike—to tell me that Paul had died. I'd never met Paul, but the news saddened me for days. It was the first AIDS death that was near to me: a lover's lover. I found myself thinking once again about wills and insurance policies, and how much time I still had; but Simon eventually shook me out of this mood. I made an appointment with my solicitor, and rewrote my will—leaving everything I owned to Simon. My cousin, I decided, couldn't really object; he, too, was gay, and for all I knew had willed his possessions to his lover.

Mike and Danny, Robert said, were settled, content, and serene in their country cottage, and thoroughly enjoying their work at the school in Stowmarket. They sent their "regards". Not "love", I noted, nor a wish for me to write or call: mere "regards". Presumably my retort to Mike about who Danny had been in bed with that afternoon had not stirred up any real trouble. Mike, perhaps, had not taken it seriously, just thought it a typical piece of gay bitching: had maybe not even mentioned it. He was, I guess, conceited enough to believe that Danny wouldn't dream of looking at another man. I never heard anything more from either of them. It's possible they lived happily ever after: shiatsu, poetry, and red roses. But I doubt it.

One of the most welcome developments of the spring and summer was the rapprochement between me and Katya. She called me one day in April and invited me to dinner at Il Fàro; she'd pay this time, she said, and Kim would *not* be there. "But bring Simon if you like," she added. "I'd love to meet him." I didn't. Our first coming together, I thought, after so long and so much that was damaging, should be between just the two of us.

I was able to eat properly on this occasion, and realised how good the food was. To make up for what I hadn't enjoyed on Kim's birthday, I ordered the same menu— salmon hollandaise, with zabaglione to follow. It was excellent.

Conversation at first was polite but difficult. I wasn't prepared to be conciliatory, though she was. We discussed everything apart from the real problem, and when she mentioned Kim, I moved the talk sideways, or back, to another topic. The wet weather, my work, the litter on Islington's streets, Simon, my new house, Chekhov (she was three quarters of the way through her book, and fairly satisfied with the progress she was making) steered us through the whole meal. The wine, the food, and her very evident desire to end our quarrel, thawed me: not enough to unlock my powers of speech on the subject of Kim-and-Katya, but enough to make me feel I *should* be able to talk about it.

"You'll come back to Alameda Street for a drink," she said, as we left the restaurant.

"Not if *he's* there."

"He isn't."

"Oh?" I was silent for a few moments, but curiosity was too strong. "Where is he, then?"

"I got him a rail pass, and he's taken a trip to the North of England. He wanted to see York Minster, and Durham, and a bunch of castles you have up there."

"Illiterate gardener jock turned culture vulture."

"Yes. Our influence on him isn't wholly bad." I said nothing to that. "Well . . . are you coming in for a drink? I have some genuine Russian vodka, the real McCoy. I've been saving it for you . . . oh, since Christmas; Anne brought it . . . you're the only person I know who'd appreciate it."

I laughed. "Except yourself. How've you been able to resist the temptation to open it?"

"Not easily."

"I'll come, then. Sure."

"Sure you're sure?"

Old dialogue patterns were now returning. "Sure I'm sure I'm sure. And we'll drive there. I got a parking ticket last time; remember?"

The Alameda Street living room was precisely as it had been, imprinted with Katya: papers, coffee cups and vodka bottles everywhere, cat fur on the chairs, books strewn all over the floor. Mess with method in it. Not a sign that Kim lived here too. No frisbee, no sweat-band. It was as if Los Gatos had been uprooted whole, and dumped in Islington. It melted the ice just that much more; as I sat beside her sipping vodka—an excellent brew, the real McCoy indeed—I said, "You stole my lover."

"Davy, Davy." She shook her head; there were tears in her eyes. "Does it help to say I'm sorry? I guess it doesn't. Do you think I haven't gone over the hurt I've done to you . . . oh, a thousand times? Searching for ways to repair it. And not finding them. Jesus . . . I've missed you these months!"

"You didn't exactly . . . *steal* him. I have to admit that."

"No," she said. "I didn't. He came of his own accord. But . . . I could have sent him back."

"He wouldn't have come."

She nodded. "That's true, too."

"And now I have Simon."

"Does that heal? Lessen the hurt?"

"Of course."

"Can you forgive me?"

"I suppose," I said, "there really isn't anything to forgive. *He* fucked it up. He and *only* he. You just happened to be around at the right moment for him. But if you hadn't been here, if you'd spent your sabbatical in Buenos Aires or Dar-es-Salaam, he'd have left me just the same."

"No. He's here because I am. He'd never have come to England if I hadn't come . . . he wouldn't be HIV positive."

"Tangled, isn't it! And if I didn't know I was . . . I'd have unwittingly made him so next time I went to California."

"Which reminds me . . . when *are* you returning to California? Have you thought about it at all?"

"I'm considering whether to do another year's exchange. Simon's never been to America; he'd love to go. He's said that . . . on several occasions."

"If you decide on San Jose again I can easily fix it. Oh, do so! And share my house as usual; Simon too, of course."

"Not . . . Katya . . . your house. I couldn't. With Kim there."

"I'm sorry! Jesus! That was dumb!" She sighed. "Yes, yes . . . you're right. It wouldn't work out. But how can I have you in California not living with me? It would be so strange . . . so weird! My punishment, I guess." She stood up and refilled our glasses.

"Not a punishment, Katya. Don't think of it in those terms. Please!"

"But where would you live?"

"I could exchange houses . . . and cars . . . with whoever did my teaching at Queen Charlotte."

"Fred Muldoon . . . do you remember Fred? . . . he wants to do a year in England. He has a very nice place in Saratoga . . . with a swimming pool." She grinned. "I could come over and use it!"

I laughed. "You are such a wire-puller," I said. "Witch!"

"I have my spells."

Another vodka, and then I said I must go. "I'll call you tomorrow. Thank you for a *really* good evening. I'll see you again . . . in a day or two."

"Do I get to meet Simon next time?"

"Sure!"

Was she deliberately at her best—wise, entertaining, relaxed, enthusiastic, as good a listener as talker; the sympathetic, winsome slightly larger-than-life Russian turned American: did she think she had—metaphorically speaking—to seduce Simon? Or was it just a natural and immediate rapport, the inexplicable chemistry which makes some people, after only a few hours, feel as if they've known one another for years? Whatever; it didn't matter. She and Simon got on so well I was almost left out. The omens beforehand had not looked good. "I'm certain I won't like her," he'd said.

"Why?" I asked.

"Because of the things she's done to you! It's obvious!"

"I said to her . . . there was nothing all that reprehensible. Nothing that needed . . . forgiveness."

"Honestly, David! Why don't I get exasperated with you? She does not come out of that particular imbroglio in *any* favorable light!"

"She ran off with my lover, you mean?"

"Yes."

"It isn't quite true."

"You call me a healer. A saint. It's absurd! *You* are! *You* are! Well . . . let's get on with it. Though don't expect me to enjoy myself."

We met her in the Spaniards pub in Hampstead for lunch, and afterwards we walked for an hour on the heath. Then visited Highgate Cemetery, and stared at the tombs of the famous (Karl Marx, George Eliot, Radclyffe Hall, etcetera) and the tombs of the rich, the absurd, and the dotty. When Katya suggested dinner that evening at Alameda Street, I did not reply, merely looked at Simon; who unhesitatingly said, "I'd love to! Is that O.K., David?"

On our own at last—about one a.m., driving from Islington back to Stoke Newington—Simon said, "I think she's wonderful. Don't laugh!"

For I was laughing so much I could scarcely steer the car straight. "All that shit you threw out this morning about being *determined* not to like her!"

He wriggled in his seat. "I wasn't *determined*; that's not the right word. But yes . . . I can understand what you see in her! I . . . I hope there'll be more days like this."

There were. We gradually resumed the old rituals— meals out, meals in, the occasional hour in a pub. We were a threesome: Kim was never present, never mentioned except when I asked where he was; "at home", or "at the cinema" were the usual replies, though one answer astonished me, indeed hurt me. It wasn't deliberate; Katya wouldn't have been aware of the significance. "Dancing the night away at the Hippodrome," she said.

"It's a bit odd," Simon said to me, one morning at breakfast, "that we *never* once saw Kim when we went out with Katya. It's . . . artificial."

She had gone. Chekhov was typed and delivered to the publishers; Alameda Street was empty and waiting for its owner to return from India; and Katya was somewhere in Connecticut, staying with friends who owned a huge Gothic mansion on the sea-shore. Kim, presumably, was with her.

"I want it to remain like that. Are you . . . curious about him, then?"

"Oh, yes, of course I'm curious. Though I don't particularly want to meet him. No!"

"Enough on Kim. I've had something more interesting in the mail."

"What?"

"It's from Professor Muldoon, finalising the exchange. We'd better get on and book our tickets for San Francisco International! Are you . . . looking forward to it?"

"You do ask silly questions! You know I am!"

He was perhaps looking forward to it more than I was; for him the experience would be entirely new, whereas I had grown a bit blasé about America. It would be the third time I was doing this exchange: at my age, living out of a suitcase for a year was, to put it mildly, not as thrilling as when I was twenty. And we hadn't been long in this house—I was growing into it, and didn't want to leave it. Nor would there be the excitement of a reunion with Katya, the gossip of twelve months to repeat and to listen to; we'd lived the twelve months instead. But she'd be there of course, which would be fine, and, I said to myself, I'd get a great deal of pleasure from showing Simon my old haunts. I hadn't previously been to California with a lover. That, instead of risking myself, alone, in Castro, in AIDS-conscious 1987: it couldn't be at all a bad thing! I poured myself another coffee, lit a cigarette, and, remembering I wouldn't have to pay income tax on my salary while I was in America, told myself I'd probably enjoy the year very much.

Simon could often read my mind. "We can always come back for Christmas," he said. "You get a six-week break, don't you?"

I smiled. "Would you want to come back here for Christmas?"

"If you're homesick . . . "

"You're sweet. And thoughtful. And I can read you too; I'm sure you don't want to be in England at Christmas, not one little bit! We could go to Hawaii, if we have the money, or . . . Los Angeles . . . Seattle . . . stay with friends in San Francisco; we're sure to be asked!"

He kissed me, and said, "I can't wait!"

"The arrangements with your school . . . no problems likely?"

"They're giving me a year's unpaid leave of absence, as you know. All I have to do is to tell them I definitely want it . . . which I will this morning." He looked at his watch. "If I don't leave sooner than now, I'll be late!"

I thought I'd ring Katya with the news. But I couldn't, I remembered; she was in Connecticut and I didn't know the phone number. I sent a postcard instead, addressed to Menlo Park.

Katya's sabbatical had come and gone: it seemed as if it were yesterday she was arriving at Heathrow, on a hot summer morning like this one. The year had hardly been what I'd anticipated. I'd moved house, and I was with a different man. Utterly unexpected! Katya-and-me had been shaken to its foundations. Unbelievable! And the virus, of course: origin of it all. But a year is often like that, I said to myself. As you get older, the unexpected occurs more frequently, not less; which is quite contrary to everything you're brought up to believe. What of a year from now? Impossible to imagine.

September; I was once again Visiting Professor at San Jose. The Muldoons were in our house in Stoke Newington, and we were in theirs in Saratoga, the next town up the highway from Los Gatos. I'd been adamant about not staying at Katya's (she was now back in Menlo Park) while Kim was there. And he was very much there—that relationship was turning out to be as strong as me-and-Simon. He, too, had not become ill; like me, he was an asymptomatic carrier. Katya had also been tested, and was antibody negative.

As in London, my life in California with Simon revolved mainly around being at home, though we were planning various trips, the tourist things: Mendocino, Carmel and Monterey, Big Sur, Los Angeles, Sacramento, and a week in Yosemite and Death Valley. And we went to San Francisco quite often—it was only fifty miles away, a mere commute in American terms—for the Golden Gate, cable cars, Alcatraz, etcetera. And a stroll or two in Castro. Simon wasn't particularly enamoured of Castro, and I—I could take it or leave it. Now.

The house was modern, and compared with our London abode, very de luxe. It had all kinds of kitchen gadgets we didn't possess, and the swimming pool was superb: Katya, as she'd said she would, took frequent advantage of this. There were two almost brand new Ford Mustangs, which were great fun to drive. (Professor Muldoon had my somewhat less elegant Toyota, and his wife had Simon's old Audi.) The garden, like those in Los Gatos, gradually merged with somebody else's, the edges vague. No palms, however; the trees were firs of various sorts, and pines and cypresses: the woods stretched up a steep mountainside. Saratoga was pristine and beautiful. It had escaped the fire.

« THIRTEEN »

Dinner at Katya's. I wouldn't have accepted the invitation if Kim was going to be there, but he was away for the night, in San Francisco. He needed these occasional expeditions, Katya said, and she didn't mind, so long as the sex was one hundred per cent safe, and he returned precisely when he said he would.

"O.K., so he does nothing he shouldn't do," I said. "But what about all the other risks? The pox, hepatitis . . ."

"And I"—she repeated the quaint mixed metaphor she'd invented once before—"could get run over by the Clapham omnibus. Maybe, as we're in Menlo Park, we should call it the Palo Alto Greyhound."

"David has become a moral conservative," Simon said. "Moral Republican?"

Katya laughed. "Freshen his drink; I guess his thirst for vodka hasn't changed. I've never known anyone, *ever*, who can swill down so much of the stuff and not get pie-eyed."

"Except yourself," I said.

"Sure." She rattled what remained of the ice cubes in her glass. "Fix mine, Simon, while you're at it." She grinned at me as he left the room. "You're a neat pair, you two. The neatest pair, David, you've ever been in."

Dinner was Katya at her most inventive: chicken stewed with artichoke hearts, asparagus and grapes, and served with a cream sauce, spinach, and pecan nuts, followed by persimmons pudding. When I asked where she had got the persimmons (they didn't usually ripen till November), she said they were last year's preserved— Kim had obtained them from someone he worked for, and bottled them. Katya had found him employment very easily in Menlo Park; "People here, many of them, are stinking rich," she said. "A gardener is an invaluable status symbol. As it is to the de los Rioses."

The wine, too, was no ordinary plonk (Ernie's California chablis at five dollars a gallon), but an expensive red from the Ridge vineyard, and a sweet white Zinfandel from which she had—or maybe she hadn't—forgotten to remove the price tag, ten dollars fifty. All this was yet another signal that the war between us was over. It wasn't just a truce, or a prelude to better relations, but peace had broken out—we were as we had been. That was fine, I decided as we sat on the deck in the hot summer dusk, drinking more vodka, reminiscing about old times, discussing books and music, relating scandal about mutual friends: just fine. My autograph on the peace treaty was as sincere as hers.

"I guess you guys had better stay here tonight," she

said. "I don't want to break up the party—but State laws on drunk driving have gotten pretty strict."

Simon, slumped in his chair, Redford purring on his lap, nodded.

"Sure," I said.

"I made up the bed in the spare room just in case." She refilled the glasses.

"Do you still think old friends are better than lovers any day of the week?"

She laughed. "I may be putting you in the shit with Simon, but I have to defend myself: it was *you* who said that. I queried the 'any'. And you conceded that the lover should have an occasional hour."

Simon grinned, and opened his mouth to reply; but decided against it. He was too sleepy. He returned to stroking the cat.

"I was very definitely wrong," I said.

"So you were. I agreed with you at the time, but I've become a revisionist too. Don't you think . . . to have the lover *and* old friends is about as satisfactory as human beings could wish for?"

"Yes. Oh . . . yes!"

A noise from indoors startled me: a key turning in a lock. "Kim," she said. She hastily lit a cigarette, to cover up, I imagine, any give-away expression on her face.

"You planned this!" I accused.

"Did I?"

"I also said you were a witch, Katya. I hope this time you've cast your spells correctly."

"Oh . . . I have!"

He came out on the deck, holding a glass of beer (the
no alcohol policy had evidently been abandoned), and
said, "Hi, everyone. Hi, David." Twenty minutes of rather stiff conversation followed, mainly about the weather,
the meal we had just eaten, and where he had been that
evening—not in San Francisco, but in downtown Campbell,
enjoying two horror movies. A great bargain, he said; you
could watch them both for only seventy-five cents.

I had drunk too much, and was in too good a mood to
be angry with Katya for engineering this situation, but I
felt extremely ill at ease. How typical of her it was to try
and organize, arrange, manipulate! Kim and Simon were
also obviously far from happy. They looked at each other
from time to time, asking themselves, I guess, what was it
David saw in this man, what did this man see in him?
Simon's not nearly so attractive as me, Kim could have
been thinking; Kim's a dull, boring person Simon might
have concluded. They said very little to each other dir-
ectly, apart from common politenesses. "What do you
think of California?" Kim asked.

"Hot," Simon replied.

"It was hot in England last August."

"It is occasionally," Simon agreed. He was still
stroking Redford. I moved my chair closer to his, then took
his hand and squeezed it. He smiled at me, gratefully.

Kim noticed this, but he did not react, apart from a
slight widening of his eyes. He was, I thought, being conciliatory; he was not deliberately attempting to show off
his sexiness. And Simon was not prepared to play the
saint—to be excessively friendly and outgoing: one false

move on Kim's part and I felt he would say something rude. Would it matter if he did? No, I decided; it wouldn't. Nothing could change what had happened in the past, and the present scene wouldn't affect my relationship with either Katya or Simon, whatever was said.

"How do you like the swimming pool at Saratoga?" Kim asked.

"A godsend in this weather," I answered.

"I'll be over tomorrow to use it," Katya said.

"While I sweat my guts out digging up potatoes," Kim said, laughing.

"I hear you once had a rather nasty accident with a swimming pool," Simon said.

"What? Oh . . . mmm . . . yes. The Smrkovskys." Kim laughed again, but he sounded nervous this time.

"The dead dog."

Katya evidently thought a hasty change of subject was needed. "I'm going to do the dishes," she announced. "Anyone want to help me?"

"I will," Simon answered, unceremoniously dropping the cat onto the deck. I wanted to say don't leave me alone with Kim, but I didn't know how. "Don't be too long," Simon whispered, as he stood up and brushed my hand.

When we were alone, Kim said, "Gee, David! There's not much light out here . . . but you're looking *sensational*! As always!"

"So are you." I had often wondered, should we ever meet by chance, whether I'd notice the differences a year's experience of living with the virus might cause him. Would it age his face, deepen a line here, allow a blond curl to fall out there, fatten him, thin him? Would there still be enough characteristics of his personality, movements of his body, the smile, the eyes glinting, the bulge in his jeans, to stir me? Oh, yes: he was more attractive than my memory, or even my fantasies, had led me to imagine.

"I love you," he said. "I miss you. If only . . . I hadn't gotten so freaked out. If only you'd been able . . . to listen to me . . . "

"Are you still freaked out?"

"No. No. Not so much. But I still go to a shrink . . . it's dirt cheap, two dollars an hour . . . it's a special AIDS suppport deal."

"Are you happy?"

"I'm O.K. And you?"

"Yes, I'm happy."

"David . . . are we going to die?"

"It's the only sure thing there is," I said, avoiding the question.

"You know what I mean."

"Are you so unfreaked as you tell me? It doesn't sound like it. Kim . . . I don't know if we'll die . . . of AIDS. So far . . . so good."

He nodded. "That's it for me, too," he said.

A long silence, not an uncomfortable one. Then we talked about his work, the places I'd been to in California with Simon, the house in Saratoga—I didn't, however, say he should come and visit—and his memories of what had impressed him most in England. Then another silence. "We ought to go in," I said. "They'll be wondering what we're doing!"

"Kiss me. Please. For old times' sake."

Not a dry kiss: he'd solved that problem too. I tried to make it gentle and sweet, but it was . . . electrifying. His hands explored my chest, reached down, found my cock. I did the same. We were rigid. "You'd better use that on Katya," I said.

He laughed, and said, "Sure!"

She was noisily banging pots and pans about. "Where's Simon?" I asked her.

"In bed. He was sleeping on his feet."

But he was in fact very much awake. "Was it difficult?" he said.

"No." I undressed—my cock had subsided—and, slipping between the sheets, I wrapped myself round him as usual. "It was difficult for you, though. That was obvious! What did you think . . . how did you feel?"

"I . . . I saw a very sexy hunk of a man."

"And?"

"O.K. It was bad . . . I'm sorry I was a bitch about the swimming pool and the dog. I felt . . . awkward. Angry that he's here. That's why I went indoors to help with the dishes."

"I'm sorry."

"I can't see us ever going around as a happy quartet. Can you? That's what Katya would like. It's what she's trying to . . . to construct. David . . . you still fancy him. I know that."

"I prefer chicken and artichoke hearts, persimmons pudding, and vintage Zinfandel."

"That's not true."

"Simon . . . nothing on earth, absolutely *nothing* on earth, is going to make me damage what you and I have. I think we are . . . a fucking *miracle!*"

"Yes. I think it's O.K. You curling round me at night . . . I feel . . . safe. I love you. Davy, Davy."

I went back to Los Gatos one afternoon—alone, which I wanted to be, though I did ask Simon if he'd like to come. Maybe he guessed I'd prefer to be on my own, for he invented various excuses: he had groceries to buy, he needed to cook, wanted to finish the novel he was reading. And it was too hot: the nearness of the Muldoons' swimming pool was a splendid reason for not doing anything energetic in the torrid September weather—California's sultriest month, the temperature in the high nineties every day.

The de los Rioses and the Smrkovskys were back, their houses rebuilt, their gardens restored. The Smrkovskys had a new swimming pool and a new dog; the pool was much like the old one, the plastic do-it-yourself variety, but the dog was quite different. Not a nervous, howling red setter, but a yapping, snapping, miniature poodle called Za-Za. (I discovered its name because Mrs Smrkovsky, more obese than ever, a hippopotamus— "G-ross!!" Katya would say—came to the door to feed it.) I did not speak to the Smrkovskys, who were never my favorite human beings, but I did chat for a moment with the de los Rioses who were, as always, unaffected and polite.

"The fire insurance money was lavish," Mr de los Rios said. "Lavish! The Smrkovskys bought that new pool with some of their share—so the palm tree fiasco didn't cost me a cent! No sir! And I never paid that guy for cutting it down! I didn't see him after the fire. What was his name?"

"Kim."

"That's right! Whatever happened to him?"

"He's living in Menlo Park."

"That's a fair distance," Mrs de los Rios said. "I guess he wouldn't want to travel up here. But gardeners aren't all that easy to find nowadays—even bad ones."

They asked how Katya was. Well, I said; her book on Chekhov was coming out next spring, and she was in California, living somewhere north of San Jose. I didn't want to say Menlo Park a second time; the de los Rioses didn't need to speculate if she and Kim were lovers.

Her house was still a charred ruin. The owner hadn't returned from Japan, and the de los Rioses didn't know what he intended to do with it. I spent some time walking through the roofless rooms; there were bits of furniture scorched by the fire or mouldy from the winter rains—the settee I'd sat on, sometimes slept on, the legs of the dining-room table, a cupboard in which a bird had made its nest. Vandals had scribbled on the walls: *Up the I.R.A.; Tom screwed Lucy 2/20/87.* I looked for some memento of Katya, but there was nothing.

The garden was a wilderness, the grass several feet high, but roses were in bloom, and poppies and belladonna lilies. No need now for Katya to worry about dried lions' urine to protect her flowers; there were no sweet peas, marigolds, nasturtiums, petunias and antirrhinums to protect. But the deer had visited—their droppings were everywhere. And around the tangerine tree, which the fire had left untouched, the humming birds were out in full force. The weight of this year's fruit had broken some of its branches; rotting tangerines littered the ground.

I ploughed on through the grass and the shrubs, many of which had been destroyed in the fire, so it wasn't difficult to make a trail. Into the clearing where Kim's cottage, the two-roomed wooden shanty, had stood. All that was left of it was ash. Here we'd drunk wine on scented summer nights. Made ecstatic love. I searched carefully through the ash, and found a frisbee. It had been melted by the fire into a peculiar pear-like shape. The one he'd been throwing the day I first saw him? Probably. And not far from it were the remains of a sweat-band.

I picked up these two relics and looked at them: I'd keep these for ever. David's "for evers." And found myself in tears. What was I mourning? Something I didn't have with Simon, that I'd never have with him, but which Kim and I had possessed: innocence. Our sex life may have been unrestrained and adult, but there was an extraordinarily innocent joy about it, about him-and-me, about *him.* The virus had not killed us, but it had killed that, for ever.

Did I still love him? No: longing to have now what we had in the past isn't the same as loving; it can only be the same if we feel we can rebuild what has been destroyed. Which was not only impossible; it was also undesirable. Kim was too selfish, had hurt me too much, for me to regret more than our lost innocence.

I was so lucky having Simon. I thought of all the men I knew with HIV, those without lovers, the cheats like Mike (*and* Kim), the careless (Danny), ones without a sex life, the guy who had Kaposi's sarcoma; the AIDS dead and the AIDS dying; the possibility that Kim and I could be—when?—victims too; the good and the evil the test brought out in us all. I was so lucky: one of that minute percentage of the fortunate! And still I couldn't stop my tears.

> It is the blight man was born for,
> It is Margaret you mourn for.

I drove up to Saratoga, determined never to come back, determined also to hide all this from Simon. The latter was a vain aspiration; he wasn't stupid: he *knew*.

He was sprawled out by the pool, reading. "How did it go?" he asked, and shut the book.

"Fine. I found these." I held up the frisbee and the sweat-band.

He looked at them, then at me, and reached for my fingers; stroked them gently. "I do understand. I do. I know exactly what's churning away inside you . . . You've been crying."

"I don't want to talk about it." I was crying again: once it begins, it isn't easy to stop—catharsis; the letting go of everything bad that had occurred since the fateful morning when Mike phoned and Kim was in the shower: *Love, O careless love.* "I feel . . . ashamed," I said.

He stood up, and held me in his arms. "I know . . .

what he was to you. What he *is* to you. I can never replace
that. No two relationships are ever alike. And . . . we
aren't perfect human beings. Who is?"

"But Simon, you are!"

"The sooner you stop that nonsense the better. I'm
not some kind of saint: I'm as faulty as you. See me as I
really am." He slipped his hands under my shirt, then
down to my cock. "We need some soothing balm. Let's
go to bed."

"I thought when I was driving back from Los Gatos I
could hide it all from you. A silly idea."

"Hide what?"

"Mourning. Grief. It should have occurred ages ago,
I guess . . . but it didn't. Well . . . it's happened now.
That's good. It's right and proper."

"David . . . he was a wildly unsuitable person. Immature . . . without compassion, empathy, incapable of
giving. A taker. He demanded things: security, excitement, money to spend, fatherly wisdom. That kind of kid
takes to his heels as soon as the first crisis looms. He
didn't love you. All he felt was the pleasure of being flattered. Flattered because a man like you thought he was
wonderful."

"The sex was pretty good," I said.

"So what?"

"Yes. So what. Anyway . . . "

"It's over?"

"Yes. This is a turning point, Simon . . . Kim is
dead and buried. I've been crying because of a death.
Now . . . there's only the future. You and me. That's

my commitment . . . you and me. And it's *total*."

"Show me," he said. "Show me in bed! Make love to me as you've never done to anyone *ever* before! Fuck me stupid! Fuck the living daylights out of me! It's what I've always wanted and never had!"

It was the wild wrestling I'd longed for with him and not dared try; the screwing that proved immortality, destroyed distress: Death, where is thy sting? Grave, thy victory?

A very elongated condom, the teat full and heavy. We lay there absolutely still. Exhausted. Drained. Covered with sweat. Fucked stupid. The smile on his face was radiant.

We both fell profoundly, dreamlessly, asleep.